H⊕RIZ⊕N

S⊕UL GUARDIANS

* B⊕⊕K THREE *

More books by Kim Richardson

SOUL GUARDIANS:

Marked Book # 1
Elemental Book # 2
Horizon Book # 3
Netherworld Book # 4
Seirs Book # 5
Mortal Book # 6

MYSTICS :

The Seventh Sense Book # 1

SOUL GUARDIANS

* BOOK THREE *

HORIZON

BY
KIM RICHARDSON

For Jacques

Chapter I
Forgotten

Kara Nightingale sat on a cold stone floor. She felt numb and empty, drained of all feeling. She could hear a frayed chorus of distant moans from the other prisoners, and she wondered when she would start having hallucinations herself. She didn't want to lose her mind to shadows in the perennial darkness of her prison cell. The voices of the dead and the forgotten were her only companions.

Over time, the jagged grey walls had become a comfort to her. She'd had no visitors since the archangel Zadkiel himself had brought her to the prison and thrown her in the cell. He had ridden on the back of one of the great eagles, like a knight riding on a powerful steed. She had dangled below in the bird's sharp talons, like a prey ready to be eaten. Zadkiel had been the last person she had seen, and she wondered if she'd ever see another soul again.

Kara sighed. She grabbed a sharp pebble and turned to face the wall behind her. She reached up and pressed the rock into the stone with just enough pressure to make a small indent and form a rough line. She sat back on her heels and admired her work. Each mark accounted for one day.

She counted twenty-eight tiny marks. She wasn't sure if her calculations were correct; it was hard to determine time in Horizon, because darkness surrounded her all the time, and she never saw the light of day. But she figured it was about right, give or take a few days. But what did it matter anyway? Angels were not mortals. Time had an entirely different significance in Horizon. Her very first assignment as a guardian had taught her that.

Her throat tightened. She remembered the first time she had been locked up in Tartarus. She could see David's smiling face when he had come to rescue her and had stood at the threshold of her prison cell. Her *knight in shining armor*, he had said. But no one had come for her this time. She had been locked up for nearly a month, forgotten like an old pair of shoes.

It wasn't doing her any good to dwell on the past.

She was amazed she was still sane. The insane moans and howls of her neighbors led her to believe that there were at least a dozen others in here, locked away on separate levels. *How many levels and cells were there in all of Tartarus?* She could only guess — thousands perhaps. She wondered how long the other prisoners had been left to fade away until their minds couldn't tell the difference between reality and illusion. How long until she began to moan and wither away? Perhaps counting the days kept her mind functioning and sane.

She burned with the desire to speak to the council and claim her innocence once more. It kept her going. She hoped that one day soon she could stand up to them and prove once and for all that she wasn't a demon spy, but a regular teenage angel, if such a thing existed. She wasn't the enemy they accused her to be. They could trust her. She was one of the good guys, wasn't she?

Kara sat back. Her head smashed against the hard wall. She knew she had really made a mess of things. She had nearly killed a fellow guardian. Then, she had escaped from Tartarus, without waiting for her trial. She had forgotten her mandate to save the mortals and had been preoccupied with a selfish quest to save her mother's soul. She had become an angel vigilante, an outcast from the supernatural world. What the council would do with her now, she could only guess. Though she knew it was going to be very unpleasant ...

With a sigh, Kara let her head fall on her knees. She remembered the evil grin on archangel Zadkiel's face. Dust and small debris had fallen from the ceiling and into her eyes when he slammed her prison door shut. His eyes had gleamed with gratification. Broad wrinkles, like potato chips, had formed on the top of his bald head. His deep-set black eyes and heavy brows had mocked her. She remembered wondering why he looked so satisfied. It seemed to her that the archangel had a personal vendetta against her and couldn't wait till she was locked up. Zadkiel had ignored her pleadings to take her straight to Gabriel. He had ignored her information about Asmodeus's plans . . . she wasn't even sure he had heard her at all. It was as though he had become deaf. He wanted nothing more than to shut her up, throw her in prison and be rid of her for good.

Kara swallowed her resentment. She shook her head. "I'm so screwed—"

"Not yet."

Kara froze. She strained her ears and realized the voice came from the wall behind her.

"Who's there? Who said that?"

Kara turned around on her knees and faced the wall. Closer inspection revealed a large crack like a lightning bolt in the jagged rock. The voice came through there. She edged closer to it.

"You need to get out of here, Kara," said the raspy voice through the fissure.

Kara imagined that the voice belonged to an elderly man. The image of Merlin, the wizard with wispy white hair and a scruffy white beard that brushed the floor, popped into her head. "You need to stop Zadkiel before it's too late."

"What—? Who are you? And how do you know my name?" asked Kara. Her lips brushed the sharp rock wall. She strained to see through the crack, but she was faced with only a shadow.

There was a moment of silence, and then the man spoke again.

"I heard the guards talk about you before. I know you are the guardian angel, Kara Nightingale. I also know that you are different from most angels, and that you possess unique and incredible powers, powers that frighten and anger the High Council. You have many enemies in the Legion, my dear."

Kara heard the stranger clear his voice, and then he spoke again. "I understand this is your *second* time in Tartarus, and that you are Asmodeus's daughter."

Kara flinched at the last words. It was strange to her how the man had said it so matter of factly, as if it was common knowledge amongst all the prisoners. She found herself wondering if this man was another nut job and if some of his sanity still remained. Would he be the kind of nut case that never shuts up and keeps rambling on forever? Would his ramblings accompany her till the end of time or until she lost her mind all together? He knew who she was. Perhaps the other prisoners weren't so insane.

"My name is Legan," said the stranger. His voice was soft and kind, not at all the tone of a rambling madman.

He continued, "… and what I have to tell you now is very important. You have to promise to tell the council *exactly* what I'm about to tell you. You cannot forget a single detail. Promise me, Kara."

Kara straightened. She couldn't help but be astonished at what she heard. "Um … nice to meet you, Legan. But what are you talking about? What is it exactly you want me to tell the council? It's not likely I'll ever get out … so you might be wasting your time. I have a feeling I'll be stuck in here for a very, very long time."

Kara heard the shuffling of feet, and then a soft plop. She knew Legan had just sat with his back against the wall. She pressed her cheek against the wall and felt a cool tingle against her angel skin. The prisoner was silent again behind the wall. Kara wondered if he was preparing his next words carefully, to try and persuade her somehow.

"You need to tell the council," said Legan finally, "that Zadkiel is a *traitor*," he hissed.

Kara noticed the disgust in the pronunciation of Zadkiel's name, as though the name itself rotted in his mouth. She had never liked the archangel Zadkiel; he had always made her feel unwelcome and grotesque. He had called her demon filth more than once. Kara smiled and felt an immediate empathy towards Legan for hating Zadkiel, too. Perhaps they could be friends?

"Never liked him," announced Kara. "He always gave me the creeps. A traitor you say? Are you sure?" She crossed her fingers. "You got proof?"

"Not yet," answered Legan, and Kara heard the disappointment in his tone. "He has all the council fooled. But *I* wasn't fooled. I know which master he truly serves. That's why I ended up here. He knew I was on to him. He had to get rid of me, you see. I was about to reveal his *mark*."

Kara shivered at the mention of the mark. The demon mark was the symbol of loyalty to the demon lord who had made it. A nasty angry scar, a demon's mark, like a spider's web, had wrapped around her ankle once. The entire Legion had accused her of being a demon spy because of it. David had pulled away from her when he saw it. Her chest tightened when she recalled his angry and confused face when she had shown him her ankle. She had just brushed it off as if it were nothing. She could never have imagined the chaos it would cause later on. Although the archangel Raphael had removed her mark, she couldn't remove the distrust it had caused. The damage had been done; she knew some angels would never trust her ever again.

"Where is he marked?" asked Kara abruptly, her voice higher than she would have wanted. She couldn't imagine where the mark would be on him. Clearly, it was cleverly concealed.

"I do not know," said Legan, and Kara heard him sigh. "The mark is hidden well on him. How he managed to conceal it, I cannot tell though he must be using some sort of illusion to mask it. A cloaking device of some sorts, I am not sure. But I know he is marked!"

Kara bit her lip. She questioned Legan's story. Maybe Zadkiel had locked up the old man, and he wanted to get back at him somehow. Getting involved with a madman couldn't help her present situation, she knew. With a sigh of resignation, she pushed herself off the wall slowly and sat back down with her back against the jagged rock. She didn't want Legan to hear.

"You do not believe me," Kara heard Legan say after a few minutes of silence. "You think I'm a crazy old fool, don't you? You believe I made this all up."

"I don't know what to believe anymore. If you have some issue with Zadkiel—that's your problem. I have enough problems of my own. I don't need this right now. Maybe you should ask someone else to help you out."

Kara threw a stone against the opposite wall. She hung her head.

"I cannot ask anyone else. You are the only one. This is *your* task, and your task alone. You must believe me, Kara, when I say that only *you* can do this," said Legan. Kara heard an urgency in his voice that made her feel uncomfortable. "Zadkiel didn't return your mother's soul to the Hall of Souls—"

"What!" Kara jumped to her feet and smacked her forehead on the wall of her cell. "How did you know about my mother's soul?"

She remembered the disgustingly satisfied grin on Zadkiel's face when she had given him the glass jar containing her mother's soul. She realized in a moment of horror that he hadn't smiled because he could return the soul to the Hall of Souls—he was smiling because he wasn't going to. It had given her the creeps then, now she felt a chill pass through her body. What had happened to her mother's soul?

"I knew a lot of things that went on in Horizon, my dear." Legan continued, "I've been around, let's say...for a very, very long time. Nothing gets past me—well, nothing did get past me until they threw me in here. But that doesn't matter anymore.

What matters is what you do now. Trust me when I tell you, he did not return your mother's soul."

The ground wavered slightly and Kara hung on to the walls so that she wouldn't fall over. The only happy thought that had kept her going all this time in the prison was the conviction that her mother's soul was safe amongst all the other brilliant hovering globes in the Hall of Souls. But now it was lost. She set her jaw. What a fool she had been. She was locked away in prison for absolutely nothing. Kara waited for the lightheaded feeling to pass before she spoke again.

"How do I know you're telling me the truth and not some fabricated lie from your damaged mind? How do I know you're not working with Zadkiel to get me killed?"

"You don't. You have to trust me," he said in a gentle voice.

When Kara didn't answer, Legan continued. "You must believe me, Kara. I am telling you the truth. Part of you knows I speak the truth—I can sense it."

Silence descended on the room. Kara ached to be with her mother again. If what the old man said was true, then her mother was in grave danger. She had to do something.

"What … what can I do?" said Kara, and she knew she couldn't mask the trembling in her voice. "I'm stuck here! How am I supposed to do anything? Do you know a way out of here?" Kara threw her weight against the hard wall, but it was like trying to move an elephant. She knew she couldn't break her way out. She thought about picking the lock. But was there a lock to her cell door? She didn't remember seeing one. Desperation filled her. How was she ever going to get out?

"You will not be locked up in Tartarus for long," informed Legan, as though reading her mind. "Soon you will be summoned to your hearing to face the charges laid against you before the High Council. It will not be easy, since the council has been misled by the poison from Zadkiel's mouth. But you must stop Zadkiel. This will be your only chance — *our* only chance. Do you understand? If you do not succeed, we are all doomed."

Kara felt another chill crawl up her back. She shuddered involuntarily. "What do you mean exactly?" It was bad enough that she was partly responsible for allowing demons to cross over to the mortal world. She didn't want to have the downfall of the angel world on her conscience, too. It would be too much for one soul to handle. "Uh … I'm completely lost. What is it that I'm supposed to do?"

"You must *touch* him."

Kara shook her head. "Excuse me? Are you mad? *Touch* him?"

"Yes," said Legan, "a single touch on him from you, and the mark will show itself."

Panic welled inside her breast. She couldn't see how she could get close enough to touch him. This plan was going from bad to worse. "They'll never let me get close to him. I'm the demon spawn; remember? They'll kill me if I get too close to the council. And then where will we be?"

"But you must, Kara. You must touch him and show the council whose master he's truly serving. They will believe you once the mark reveals itself. I promise."

"I don't know. This doesn't sound like a master plan." Kara let her head fall against the wall. An image of her mother's beautiful face danced before her eyes. Big-band music drifted in her ears. She remembered listening to Billie Holiday while doing the dishes with her mother as they sang along and spilled water all over the linoleum floor. Her nerves fluttered inside her. She owed it to her mother to try. "Okay. I'll do it."

"Good," said Legan, and Kara was sure he smiled. "It won't be long now."

Kara wasn't sure what he meant by that. Was this all a madman's scheme? How did he know when the council would summon her? How deep were his connections to the outside world? She had been locked up for so long that she had started to forget what it was like outside these walls. Something nagged at the back of her mind.

"Legan. Why haven't you spoken to me before? Why now?"

"Well, I wasn't *here* before. That is to say, I was in a different place."

"Like below a few levels or something?" Kara wondered just how many cells belonged to the concrete block they called a prison. It was an enormous structure. She figured it must hold thousands of cells. Were thousands of innocent angels locked away?

"Hmmm … yes … I suppose. Something of that sort," said Legan. "Here they come. Get ready, Kara. We shall meet again soon."

"What—?"

Kara heard a loud screech followed by a deafening boom. The cell walls shook, and for a minute Kara thought there might have been an earthquake, but she quickly realized that was impossible because they were floating in a giant cube. She whirled around. She wiped the dust and dirt from her eyes and blinked.

Kara stared into the piercing golden eyes of a giant eagle.

CHAPTER 2
ZADRIEL

Kara walked along the endless corridor leading to the High
Council chamber. Tall grey walls dressed with colorful
tapestries and the occasional portrait of some important angel
official surrounded her on either side. The stale air was hot, and
dust tickled her nose. Her boots echoed through the empty
corridors, cutting the eerie silence like a knife. The exquisite
wooden doors of the offices reminded Kara of the monumental
Chateau Frontenac hotel where she had spent a day exploring
the different levels on a school trip. She peered through an open
door. It was an office, she realized, and she stepped inside. It
was cluttered with papers, and books were piled all the way to
the ceiling like crooked ladders. Light leaked from a large
window at the far end, lighting up thousands of dust particles
floating in the air like miniature snowflakes. The office seemed
deserted. Kara felt uneasy. Where was everyone?

Unlike the other times she had been summoned to the
council, when the halls had been filled with curious onlookers,
this time the halls were deserted. Not even an oracle came to
greet her on the landing platform to escort her to the council, as

they always did. No one came, and she felt a nasty chill roll up her back. What was going on?

Kara walked out of the office and continued to make her way towards the council chamber. She reached out and dragged her fingers along the walls, reassuring herself that they were real, and that she wasn't back in her cell hallucinating. She wondered if she had gone mad—and this was all in her mind. Kara shook her head and pressed on. She figured that once she arrived at the council things would become clear. It would all make sense.

She spotted the giant metal doors of the council chamber at the far end of the hall. They stood before her, majestic and accusing. They judged her before she even pled her case. She walked up to them and pressed her trembling hands against the cold metal. Uncertainty flooded through her. She questioned what would happen once she entered the chamber. Would the High Council believe her now or would they simply lock her up again until she withered away, mad as a hatter. Why they had locked her away for so long, kept her guessing.

She steeled herself. She'd fight for the truth, even if it meant they'd throw her back in prison. But she couldn't forget what Legan had told her...how important he had made her feel, the hint of desperation in his voice. She had a job to do. She had to get near Zadkiel somehow. She had to touch him. Once the Mark was revealed, the council would believe her—Legan had told her so. She decided to take that chance. Legan had handed her an opportunity; she had to take it. She fought to control her nerves. She readied herself and pushed the metal doors.

The doors screeched on their hinges as she pressed them apart. She sauntered into the chamber and stopped. The great round room was empty, save for seven archangels who sat behind a glistening black desk raised on a dais at the opposite end of the room, like a giant black diamond. Yellow light spilled through the rounded glass dome above her, like an enormous greenhouse, filling the room in a soft light. Spasms erupted all over Kara's body, and she forced herself to stay calm. She didn't want the archangels to notice her fear. *Be strong.*

Kara scanned the room again quickly. Her chest tightened. David wasn't here either. She wasn't sure why she actually expected him to show up. He hadn't come to see her in Tartarus. But she wasn't even sure if visitors were allowed. They probably weren't. Maybe he had to lie low? She convinced herself that David was occupied elsewhere, or that he didn't even know her trial was today...which was really unlikely...

She set her jaw. Legan's words echoed in her head. She lifted her eyes and met Zadkiel's gaze. She flinched. His black eyes stared back at her. A mixture of satisfaction and disdain painted his face. He was searching her face, reading the fear in her eyes. His bald head stood out against his red robes, like a severed head above a bloody stump. She forced herself not to look away. She didn't want to give him the satisfaction. Hatred filled her. What had he done to her mother's soul? He would pay for this. Her chance had come. She knew exactly what she had to do.

Kara clenched her fists and walked forward. She knew the drill, and she walked over to the lonely bench conveniently placed below the council members. She figured they sat on a raised platform so that they could look down upon the poor soul who happened to be summoned—a power trip. But it was her turn now. She let herself fall onto the bench. She sat calmly with her hands on her lap and looked up. She met Uriel's eyes. She watched him raise his eyebrows, but his face was as unreadable as ever.

"Kara Nightingale," said Uriel, in a musical tone. "How delightful to see you again so soon—"

"This is soon?" blurted Kara before she could stop herself. She pressed her lips together, eyes wide. She saw annoyance flash in Uriel's perfect face momentarily, and then it was gone. His dark eyes glimmered as he studied Kara. The light from above illuminated his delicate features and silky brown hair.

"There are two serious charges laid against you." Uriel interlaced his fingers. His golden robes glistened in the light, and Kara thought he looked like a golden statue. "Both are very serious indeed, and I find myself very disappointed in you, Miss Nightingale. We had high hopes for a guardian of your special talents, who showed so much promise. We are faced with terrible times, and this is very unfortunate."

Kara stared back in puzzlement. She wasn't sure what he meant by terrible times. Had she missed out on something? Was he referring to the mass release of demons into the mortal world? She fidgeted in her seat, and tried not to feel culpable. She knew that striking Al had been an accident, but escaping from Tartarus wasn't. She hoped the council didn't know that David or the others were involved in her break out.

"The council has had time to review your cases extensively," continued Uriel, his mouth pressed in a hard line. "After listening to the eye witness accounts and reviewing the evidence in your first case, the council has voted and has found you *guilty* of the crime of attempted murder of a fellow guardian—"

"What! You can't be serious!" Kara couldn't hide the anger in her voice. She jumped up and threw her hands in the air. "It was an accident! Who are your eyewitnesses? Did you speak to David McGowan? He was there … he can tell you it was an accident. What about the archangel, Cassiel? He can tell you—"

Uriel lifted his hand to silence Kara. "We have questioned the archangel Cassiel on several occasions. He believes it was an accident … but the evidence speaks for itself. Unfortunately for you, we never found the dagger you spoke of. You viciously attacked an unarmed angel … and nearly killed him. Fortunately, he lives, the archangel Raphael mended him, so your sentence will be more lenient."

Kara trembled. Anger flared inside her. She fought to control her temper. She had run the entire scenario in her head for weeks; this was not how she had imagined it. She glowered at Zadkiel. To her surprise, his face openly showed his immense satisfaction.

"This isn't fair! This isn't a trial. Your witnesses are liars! It was an accident!" yelled Kara before she could stop herself. She felt herself losing control.

Uriel leaned closer. "Compose yourself, Miss. Without the evidence of the knife, it's your word against his." His dark eyes flickered as he studied Kara momentarily. "And from what we've gathered, you were not injured ... correct?"

"Yes, but—"

"A terrible crime was committed," continued Uriel as if he hadn't heard Kara. "One party was nearly killed, while the other party didn't even have a scratch. The eyewitnesses all say that you attacked him from the back, leaving him defenseless — without the ability to fight back. How could he have defended himself from such an attack? So tell me now, Miss Nightingale. How do you expect us to believe you when all the evidence points to you?"

Kara suppressed the scream rising in her throat. Her bottom lip trembled. She clenched her fists. "Because it's the truth. I never meant to hurt him. It was an accident. We were training ... and then Al and David started fighting. I saw him pull out a death blade ... he was going to hurt—"

"Yes, we've all heard this before." Uriel sat, poker faced, drumming his fingers on the gleaming black desk.

"Unfortunately for you, there is no blade. There was never any blade, was there? You made up this silly story to hide your crime."

Dread welled inside her. This was much worse than what she had imagined. "No, that—that's not true," she said, her voice wavering. "There was a blade! I saw it. It was black ... and it had marks—"

"Enough of your lies!" boomed Uriel. He pushed back his chair and stood up. His robes billowed before him like liquid gold. "We have voted, and the council has found you guilty. The decision is final. You are therefore sentenced to serve out your term in Tartarus ... for five hundred years."

Shock exploded in Kara—they didn't believe her. Fear ate at her core. She knew she couldn't survive even a few more months in Tartarus, let alone five hundred years. The weight of Uriel's words pulled her down, like a metal chain wrapped around her neck. The room started to spin. Kara strained to keep from fainting.

"But ..." Kara heard Uriel say, as she tried to focus. "If you give up the names of the angels that helped you escape from Tartarus ... the council has agreed to lessen your sentence."

Kara lifted her eyes. "It was just me. No one helped me." Her voice wavered, but she didn't care.

"Liar!" The archangel Zadkiel jumped up and pointed a large finger at Kara. His face screwed up in disgust. Kara stared back, wishing she could punch him in the face. "She lies! The guards told us that she had help. They saw *three* other angels. Give us their names!"

"The guards are mistaken," replied Kara, glad that her voice was even. She glowered at Zadkiel—the true traitor posing as the good guy. He made her sick. "I escaped on my own. I had no help." She remembered David's cocky expression when he had come to rescue her. It had been a great moment for both of them.

Zadkiel struck the desk before him with a giant fist, and Kara wondered how it didn't break. He leered at Kara from his seat. "How can we let this filth live and spread her lies? She is the demon lord's daughter. You are all aware of this. He created this *monstrosity* and disguised her as a girl to fool us all!"

He turned to face the council and waved his arms theatrically. "Do not be fooled by her. She is a creature of evil, a spawn of the netherworld, sent here to destroy our world. She will try and kill us all! I vote for the true death. Kill the demon. Be rid of her once and for all!"

Kara noticed Zadkiel's skin flicker to a darker shade, and then it went back to its normal olive tone. Murmurs reached her ears, and she saw some council members nodding their heads in agreement.

Once the whispers died down, a beautiful archangel woman with rolling red hair and flowing green robes said, "Let's not get in over our heads, Zadkiel." Kara recognized her immediately. She was the archangel Camael. She had always shown kindness towards Kara. And Kara wondered if Camael believed her.

"She will be punished for her crime," continued Camael. "As we have discussed previously, the true death will not be applicable in this case."

"I say that it should! We should take another vote." Zadkiel turned and faced Kara, his eyes blazing. "She should die for her crimes! We cannot let her live and corrupt other angels!"

"Enough!" roared Uriel. "We have already spent too much time discussing these cases. Kara Nightingale is a unique angel … and should be treated as such. She will not suffer the true death. The council has voted."

Uriel shared a look with Zadkiel.

Kara had the impression that they must have had this discussion many times before.

Uriel turned his attention back to Kara. "Now, Kara. If you want a lesser sentence, give us the names of your accomplices."

Kara watched Uriel's lips move. Her mouth wouldn't open. How could she betray her only friends? She wouldn't. She forced the words out of her mouth. "Like I said — I escaped on my own. I used my *unique* powers to blow down the door, and then I jumped." For a moment, Kara saw a look of surprise pass over Zadkiel's face. He seemed to have taken the bait.

"It was that David McGowan again," growled Zadkiel, his voice rising. "I'm sure it was him."

"Be quiet!" bellowed Uriel, and Kara noticed that he had lost his patience with Zadkiel. It gave her an idea.

"Why are you so intent on having me killed, Zadkiel?" asked Kara, in her most innocent voice, and tried to keep a disinterested expression.

"Because you are the demon's progeny! Sent here to trick us!" spat Zadkiel.

"Right. So, in your eyes … I'm a traitor?"

"You *are* a traitor! I've always known you were a traitor."

"I'm the traitor who saved the elemental child from Asmodeus, right? But then, tell me why did I do that? Why didn't I just give the kid to Asmodeus, if I'm a traitor?" Kara took a step forward.

"Because you are trying to deceive us into believing you are good," said Zadkiel in disgust. "You want the council to trust you, so that you can destroy them with your demon powers when they are least expecting it. But you don't fool me, demon."

Kara met Zadkiel's stare with a level gaze. "I see. So you think that I'll use my demon powers to kill everyone in this room. You're saying that I'm powerful enough to kill all of you now—" She snapped her fingers. "Like I can snap my fingers and—poof—all gone. So then why aren't I doing that now? Why am I letting myself be thrown into prison instead of killing you all and then going to hang out with my dad in the Netherworld?"

Zadkiel's jaw was a hard line. "Maybe you're waiting for better timing...or for orders from your true master."

"Don't you mean *your* true master, Zadkiel?" Kara saw recognition flash in the archangel's eyes, and wondered if anyone else had seen it too.

Zadkiel began to laugh. "Everything out of your mouth is a lie! You just can't help yourself—it's in your nature."

Kara watched Zadkiel without expression. "Isn't it *your* nature to serve the demon lord, your true master? You want me gone because you fear that I can kill him."

"Nonsense, the demon lord is our sworn enemy," said Zadkiel, and Kara saw his fingers twitch. "The council is in the process of planning his demise, we will—"

"—but you know that's not true." Kara's tone was casual. "You believe I can destroy him, and that's why you want me dead."

"I heard enough of her lies!" hissed Zadkiel, with a look of intense hatred. "Take her back to her cell. We can continue the deliberation later."

"I'd like to hear what else Kara has to say," said Camael suddenly. She flicked her eyes towards Kara for a moment. "If they are all falsehoods, then you have nothing to fear, Zadkiel."

"Lies from the demon's tongue! Don't listen to her." Zadkiel pushed his chair out of his way and stepped down from the dais. He strode towards Kara. His bald head glistened in the light. "Take her back! I demand she be put back into her prison!" shouted Zadkiel to no one in particular.

"Why don't you tell him about the archangel, Legan?" said Kara. "You locked him up because he found you out. Isn't that true?"

Zadkiel frowned, then threw his head back and laughed. "There is no archangel with the name Legan in Tartarus — or anywhere else in Horizon. You lying filth." He turned to the council. "You see. She lies. You all know there is no one of that name. She is delusional."

Kara saw confusion spread over the council's faces. Did she get his name wrong, she wondered. It was hard to hear from the other side of the wall, perhaps she did get his name wrong.

"Maybe I didn't get his name right, but I know what he said was true." She glared at Zadkiel. "What did you do with my mother's soul?"

Zadkiel flinched. "What are you talking about? More lies. She cannot help herself. Can't you see she is mad?"

"My mother's soul was in a glass jar. I gave it to you. What did you do with it?"

Zadkiel smiled and observed the council. Kara noticed that Uriel seemed distraught. She saw Zadkiel noticing it too as he fought to control his composure.

"I have no idea where your mother's soul is. Perhaps it is lost. What does that have anything to do with your crimes? Send her back!"

Zadkiel stood beside Kara. She could see the delicate ruby red trimmings around his large collar and sleeves. His hands twitched.

"You're the liar, and the traitor. And I'll kill you if I find out you hurt my mother."

"Ha! There she goes again. A mad demon should be locked away for good. I had enough of the filth from her mouth."

Come closer, Kara thought.

"Say hi to my father for me when you see him. I'm sure the two of you will have lots to talk about —"

Zadkiel grabbed Kara roughly by the arm and threw her down. She landed hard on the marble floors.

She grinned. She had him exactly where she wanted. This was her chance. She jumped up with incredible speed. Before Zadkiel knew what was happening, Kara had reached out and pressed her hand on his bare chest above his collar.

A puzzled expression appeared on Zadkiel's face. Kara backed away. She scanned his body for the mark. She frowned. There was nothing...Had Legan lied to her? Dread crept inside her as she took an involuntary step back.

Zadkiel laughed. He looked up at the council. "Isn't this clear enough? The girl is mad —"

Kara heard Camael gasp. She pointed to Zadkiel, horror coloring her face. "He's Marked! Look!"

Kara saw a black mark like a spider's web slowly materialize until it covered half of Zadkiel's face, like a mask.

Uriel's face was frozen in shock. "How could you? How could you betray us?"

A strange laugh escaped from Zadkiel. He smiled. Everyone was staring at him now. "Why? Why you ask? Because you are fools! Mortal-loving fools! You love the weak. It's pathetic."

Uriel glanced over to Kara; his eyes were filled with remorse. He shook his head and pointed to Zadkiel who smiled back. "You will pay for this! Summon Michael—"

Black lightening shot out of Zadkiel's hands like electric tendrils.

They hit Kara.

She rocketed back into the air and crashed into the wall. She crumpled to the floor and winced. Black smoke coiled from her body, like a smoking log. She heard a thundering roar and looked up. Millions of glass shards exploded from the sky, like sheets of glass rain and the entire room was showered in diamonds. They hit the ground in a cacophony of breaking glass. Kara caught a glimpse of a red robe dash across the room and disappear behind the chamber doors.

CHAPTER 3
DISAPPEARING ACT

After about twenty minutes of apologies and excuses from the council, for not believing Kara and locking her up in Tartarus for so long under false allegations, the High Council removed all charges that were laid against her. Kara was reinstated as a guardian angel.

Before Kara was excused, Uriel informed her that he was going to set up teams of the most dependable GAs to arrest the traitorous Zadkiel and to search for her mother's soul. But Kara answered that this was something she had to do personally. She welcomed the help, but she had to search on her own as well. Kara rushed out of the great hall with a smile on her face. She silently thanked the angel Legan for all his help. He hadn't been mad after all.

The elevator jerked to a stop. The doors slid open, and Kara stared out into a sea of ruby-red dunes. She jumped out and landed with a soft *poof* in the smooth sand of Operations. She was tickled with glee with the fresh air that caressed her face and the distant smell of salt water. How she had missed that smell. In Tartarus, the only smells had been the constant fragrance of mold and the nose-burning stench of bird droppings. She could hear the soft splashes and plops of angels jumping into the myriad of salt-water pools, heading off towards their next missions.

Kara wiped her bangs from her face and pressed on. Zadkiel had about a half hour head start, but if she pushed herself more she might catch up to him. She clenched her fists and imagined herself punching the malicious smile off his face. He wouldn't be so pretty after she was done with him. Every inch of her being screamed with the desperation she felt. Her mother's soul was lost again. She knew she couldn't fail this time. She had to find Zadkiel. Kara knew that if anyone could figure out where the traitor had gone who might help her, it was the archangel Gabriel.

With the sun blazing against her back, Kara raced down the rolling red hills. The memory of handing Zadkiel the glass jar with her mother's soul helped her gain incredible speed. Kara felt as though she was flying. Was this another super ability from her elemental powers? She didn't know— maybe it was just the anger. Either way, she couldn't tell anymore if her boots touched the sand at all.

A figure came towards her and slowed down. From the way it moved its square shoulders, she could tell it was male. He came closer. She felt goose bumps all over her body. Warmth spread through her like a hot bath. She fought to control her emotions as she looked into David's face.

He wore a pair of scruffy blue jeans with a tight black t-shirt that showed off his muscular chest. His signature brown leather jacket swayed at his sides as he walked. Clear blue eyes smiled at her. The beautiful face she had longed for and imagined so many times in Tartarus was even more beautiful close up than she remembered. With a lopsided grin, David sauntered towards her.

He stretched out his arms and lifted Kara in a tight embrace. She couldn't find any words to say and let her face dig into David's neck instead. She trembled with passion, with feelings that were forbidden in Horizon, but that were too strong to deny. She wondered if David felt the same. She didn't want to let go. The distant memory of a kiss and his hard body pressed against hers — she felt him shaking and held him tighter. Her feet dangled in the air, and David's strong arms wrapped around her affectionately.

Kara heard someone clear their throat, and then a short giggle.

"I hate to be the one to break up this happy reunion ... but we have a job to do."

David released Kara, and she turned to meet the voice. Jenny stood before them. Her short purple hair glimmered in the sunlight like a crown of purple sapphires. She had on the same black cargo pants and purple bomber jacket with the sleeves cut off that Kara remembered. Her eyes were rimmed with a thick line of black kohl, which made her green eyes stand out. Her pointy face and delicate features always made Kara think Jenny looked like a pixie.

"Can I get a hug too?" Jenny faked a pout.

"Come here you big baby." Kara pulled Jenny into a tight bear hug. "I really missed you guys."

"We missed you too."

Kara looked up. Peter bounced into view. He wore the same CDD combat outfit as Jenny. It seemed far too big for him, or was he too small for it, she wasn't sure. He pushed his glasses up the bridge of his nose. "You were gone a long time."

Kara let out a small laugh. "Well, *excuse* me for being in prison. It's not like I had any visitors or anything." She was glad her voice didn't betray the hurt she felt inside. The four lonely stone walls of her cell had not been much company for the past month.

David felt her disappointment. "I tried — we tried ... but they didn't let us."

David took a step towards Kara. His gentle eyes studied her, and Kara felt her chest tighten. "It wasn't as easy this time. We couldn't risk getting caught ... it would have made things a lot worse for you, Kara. Those douche bags had us watched constantly. We couldn't do anything without being followed."

Jenny let out a long sigh. "It was *freaking* annoying. I almost punched one in the face." Her lips twitched into a smile.

"So what happened to you, Kara?" David studied her closely, his blue eyes blazing. "I mean, a few minutes after you entered the demon realm, all hell broke loose on Earth — literally. It was as though a dark shadow passed over the world, releasing evil as it went."

A few minutes? Kara was sure she had been in the demon realm for a few hours at least. It didn't make any sense. Perhaps time had no meaning in the Netherworld. It was her only explanation.

"There were demons everywhere, attacking mortals," continued David. "It was nuts. The sun disappeared, and it became dark as night in the middle of the afternoon. We figured it had something to do Asmodeus. So, what happened in the Netherworld?"

All eyes focused on Kara. She wondered if she should tell them everything. Would they still be her friends if they knew that Asmodeus had used her to open the portals to the mortal world? How would they react once she had told them this was all her fault?

Life had been so incredibly easy for her back when she was mortal. She wasn't faced with such challenges and horrible truths about who she was. She had been a normal teenager, with the same hopes and dreams for a better life as any other teen her age. It all seemed so long ago, a memory of a dream. She knew she would never have it back.

Kara decided to tell them everything.

She described the events as best she could. She recounted everything from the giant cockroach, Jean-Pierre, leaving out the kissing parts, to the Mirror of Souls and the opening of the portals, to finally how she had barely escaped. Once she had finished, she stood with her arms crossed and waited for their reactions.

David cocked his head and shoved his hands in his jean's pockets. "You think this is your fault, don't you. I can see it on your face."

Kara hated that he could read her so easily. "You think? Of course I do. Without me, Asmodeus wouldn't have been able to open the portals." She remembered the beams of golden elemental current being sucked out of her and hitting the wall of mirrors, opening a passage for every demon imaginable to cross over into the mortal world. She shuddered at the memory.

Jenny grabbed Kara's hand and squeezed. Her face was kind. "You have to stop thinking like that. You can't blame yourself. He used you. This isn't your fault, girl."

"Jenny's right," said Peter, who Kara thought looked a little uncomfortable. "You couldn't have known about his plans. You wanted to do something good. You wanted to save your mom."

"Yeah, don't beat yourself up about it," said David, his expression thoughtful. "We'll make things right, Kiddo. I promise."

Kara hoped that they were right. She felt better telling them, but she couldn't shake off the guilt. They couldn't understand what it was like to be forced to do something terrible, with no way of stopping it. She knew it wouldn't matter how many times her friends told her it wasn't her fault, she would always feel partly responsible. She had to make things right again—no matter what the cost.

Kara forced a smile. "Well … I guess you're right. I'll try not to think of it as my fault, but I can't promise that I won't."

She noticed that David was about to reply, and she quickly cut him off. "Listen, I need to find Gabriel. I don't have much time. He has to set up a team for me to look for my mother's soul—"

"He already did," answered David, with a cheeky smile. He lifted his arms. "We're it."

Before Kara could control herself, her face broke into a smile. "I don't know how you managed that with Gabriel … but I'm glad it's you guys." She looked from one of them to the other. She couldn't have asked for a better team. She knew she could trust them with anything. "Did Gabriel fill you in about Zadkiel?" Kara spit out his name. She was surprised at her hatred.

David cracked his knuckles. "You mean that lying traitorous piece of garbage? Yeah, he told us what happened. We all know that Zadkiel was a double-crossing demon lover. He turned the council against you … and tried to have you killed. I can't wait to kick his ass." David shook his head and laughed in spite of himself.

"Okay, listen up," urged Peter, his voice louder than usual. He reached into his jacket pocket and pulled out a small contraption that looked like an iPad. He pressed his fingers against the smooth screen. "Zadkiel went through a Rift on Tartarus … near one of the entrances. If we leave now, there's a chance the Rift might still be open. But we have to leave now."

Kara felt a shiver pass through her at the mention of the angel prison. The idea of being near those grey stone walls again and hearing the dreadful incessant moans, terrified her. She could only hope it would be a fast trip. She felt a hand press against her shoulder and looked up to find David staring back at her.

"Don't worry, Kara. Those giant turkeys can't hurt you anymore. If they try anything, I'll have them plucked and ready for Thanksgiving dinner."

Kara shook her head. "The guards never hurt me. They never even spoke to me. It's the solitude that makes someone go mad." A cold spasm went through her body as she recalled the endless darkness and the eerie moaning from the other prisoners. Legan's voice echoed in her ears. A wave of shame rippled through her. She had hardly even thought about him since she left. After all, it was because of Legan that she was free now, and she hadn't even asked the council for his release. She had only thought of herself and her mother.

Her head felt heavy. "Let's get out of here."

David clapped his hands together. "All right, ladies and gents — let's do this!"

After an intense and terrifying ride to Tartarus, Kara jumped off the sky-car and landed on hard concrete. She thanked the driver for a safe trip, turned and looked up at the giant stone walls. Jagged edges like razor blades perforated the stones. No one would dare try to climb these walls to escape, they would slice away their hands and feet if they did. Without handholds to hang on, they would simply plummet to their deaths.

An opening stood before them at the other end of the platform. The entrance to Tartarus was a black rectangle, etched in darkness. It was as though a perfect piece of the wall had been cut out by giant hands. It was a small hole compared to the colossal stone cube. Kara strained to hear the cries from the prisoners. A sudden scraping sound reached her ears, and Kara looked up and saw a giant eagle pass through the entrance.

His magnificent golden feathers rippled in the soft wind like golden waves. He wore a large metal breast-plate and a metal helmet, and Kara thought that was what gave him away as a guard. A long silver chain with a glowing blue star swayed and bounced against his powerful chest. His toffee colored eyes watched Kara, and she had a feeling he wasn't so happy to see her again so soon.

"The Rift is right here." Peter pointed to the right side of the doorway, where a giant wall of rock rose up into the blue sky and disappeared within the clouds. Kara hadn't noticed it before, but now she could see a wave rolling against the wall, as though a part of rock was made of water. "This is where he passed through."

"Is this another Rift to the demon world?" David hovered before the Rift. He lifted his hand and moved it slowly above the Rift without touching the stone. "You think I can go through this one? Or is it just Kara who can pass."

Peter touched the screen on his pad. He looked up. "I don't know. I can only monitor the changes in the fields. I don't know where the doorways lead to—"

"Well, there's only one way to find out—" David plunged his arm through the Rift.

"David! No!" yelled Kara, Jenny, and Peter at the same time.

After a moment, David retrieved his arm. It was unscathed.

"Ha! Look, nothing happened!" David laughed as he paraded his arm. He started to do a dance and moved his hips in a strange way that made Kara look away embarrassed.

Jenny was pleased with this new discovery and jumped beside David. Her green eyes sparkled in delight. "So ... we all go. I wonder where it leads if not to the demon world."

"It doesn't matter where it leads, as long as it leads us to my mother." Kara studied the Rift for a moment, and then glanced over to the prison's doorway. "There's something I have to do first," said Kara. She watched Jenny pluck out one of her earrings and hand it to the sky-car's driver, who accepted it graciously. "Zadkiel had an angel locked up in here because he was on to him. He's the only reason I knew how to make his mark appear. He's the reason why I'm out. He told me how to do it. He deserves to be freed. I can't go anywhere before we do this. I owe him that much."

"Sounds good to me," said David. He turned and walked up to the guard. "Hey … big bird! Think you can get us inside to release our friend? Think you can do that? Or do I have to go and have a chat with your boss?"

The giant eagle lowered its head towards David. It regarded him for a moment before it spoke. "I have special orders to answer to *her*," he cocked his head towards Kara, and she heard David mumble something under his breath.

"Who is this friend of yours you speak of?" said the eagle.

Kara shuffled closer and looked up. "His name is Legan. He was in the cell next to mine —"

"That's impossible," said the guard.

Kara wrinkled her face and kept her composure. "I'm telling you … *he's* in there, and I want you to let him out!" She felt her temper rising and was glad for it. She wouldn't stand for his attitude. These birds didn't exactly warm her stay in the prison. She would have preferred to be treated badly, than to be forgotten altogether.

The guard ruffled his feathers in annoyance. "You are mistaken. It is impossible that your *friend* as you say was in a cell next to yours. There are no cells next to yours. You were in a high security cell, with nothing but thick walls surrounding you."

A chill passed through Kara. She wondered if she had indeed imagined the entire thing. She felt the stares of the others on her, and suppressed a shudder. What if they thought she was mad? Had she made up a friend to ease her loneliness? But then how would she have known about Zadkiel's mark? No. Legan wasn't a figment of her imagination, but a real angel who had been in the cell next to hers. The eagle was mistaken, or worse, he was lying.

"That's not true," said Kara, as she remembered Legan's raspy voice coming through the wall. "He's here. I know he is. You're lying. You're hiding something. I demand to see him at once!"

The eagle's face was expressionless. "There is no one by that name in Tartarus, and as I have told you ... there are no cells or rooms that neighbored yours. Only thick walls of stone — "

"Now you listen here, you big piece of poultry," said David and pointed to the large bird's face. "If Kara says he's in there, that means he's in there. Now let's go!"

"As you wish." The eagle turned its massive body. It bent its head and stepped through the doorway. David beckoned to Kara to follow the guard, and he stepped in after her, followed closely by Jenny and a wide-eyed Peter.

Kara stepped into darkness. Tall shadows surrounded her. A deep roar sounded from the depths of the prison, and Kara felt as though the monstrous cube was welcoming her back. Three brilliant green orbs appeared. They hovered before them like large fireflies and gave off enough light to see through the blackness. A low rumble came from the deep. The sound rose until the tremors were all around them. Kara watched as pieces of rock detached themselves from the walls to form the path below their feet as they went. It was too bad the lights couldn't mask the burning stench of bird droppings. She heard Jenny complain rudely about the smell.

The group walked in silence for a while. The light tread of their footsteps reverberated in the darkness, followed by the eerie sound of sharp talons scraping the stone floor. The prison's walls rumbled and shook with every step, as though commanding respect of all those who entered. Kara had a nasty feeling the walls could come crashing down upon them at any moment, sending them all to the black void below. She felt dreadfully uncomfortable wandering inside Tartarus again. She had hoped to forget about it, to shake it off like a bad dream.

Soon the group found themselves standing before a chamber. A large concrete door stood ajar. Kara glanced to the side nervously. There were no adjoining cells to either side. Just walls of more thick rock, she realized. Her chest tightened. What was happening?

"This isn't the same cell." Kara eyed the large bird. "This is a trick. Where's my prison cell?"

The eagle cocked his head towards the room. "This is it."

"It can't be," said Kara stubbornly. She watched the eagle's expression, and she swore he looked annoyed.

"This is it," repeated the guard.

Frustrated, Kara stomped into the tiny room...the hair on her entire body stood up. Small indents covered the back wall, spaced out equally in sections like days in a calendar. They were her marks, she realized in horror. This was indeed her cell.

Kara's mouth fell open in silent protest. "How is this possible—?"

She ran over to the back wall and pressed her hands against the sharp rock. It felt cool against her angel skin. Kara ran her fingers up and down the wall and searched for the opening from which she and Legan had shared information.

"Where's that stupid crack?" Kara frantically moved her hands all along the wall. Her fingertips tapped every inch of the rough wall, passing over every little bump and probing into every tiny hole. But she didn't find openings of any kind. It was as though the wall had swallowed up the crack.

Kara fell to her knees. "I ... I don't understand. He was here. We talked for like an hour—he told me about Zadkiel! I couldn't have made this up. It doesn't make any sense. He was real. I'm not crazy!" Kara hit the wall with her hand. "What is happening?"

"It's okay, Kara." David stood beside her. He placed his hand on her shoulder reassuringly. "No one's saying you're crazy. I'm sure there's a very good explanation—"

"The explanation is that there was never anyone on the other side." Kara heard the eagle say. Her temper flared.

Kara's hands shook, afraid of what she might do to the bird. She kept looking at the wall. "I didn't imagine this, David. He was there. I swear it."

"I believe you, Kara," said David, and Kara saw the concern in his face. She wasn't sure if it was a concerned *it'll-be-okay-face*, or a concerned *the-girl-went-crazy-face*. She figured it was the latter.

Kara's eyes flicked to Jenny who only offered a shrug and quickly looked away. Great, now her friends thought she was a mental case. But she knew the truth. Legan was real.

"Uh … guys?" Peter popped his head inside the cell. "If we want to go through the Rift and be able to come back before it closes — we have to leave now. If we don't … we won't be able to get through."

"Come on, Kara. He's right." David strolled towards the doorway. "We have to go now, or we'll lose your mother's soul for good."

Reluctantly, Kara pushed herself up and ignored her friends' stares. She knew how this scene must look to them. She had lost her sanity to the grey and lonely walls of Tartarus, and they felt sorry for her.

Kara struggled to keep her legs steady and staggered through the door. She kept her head down and avoided their eyes.

"Let's go find my mother's soul." Kara ran back to the platform. She wondered what had happened to Legan? Was he really a figment of her imagination, a temporary glitch in her brain caused by the isolation and solitude from inside the walls of Tartarus? Or did something awful happen to him? Fear welled up inside her. Perhaps it wasn't a coincidence the Rift was on Tartarus. Maybe Zadkiel came here to finish him off before disappearing back to his true master. Something didn't fit, and she promised herself that she would figure out what happened to Legan—after she rescued her mother.

Kara stood before the Rift. She felt the anxiety rising inside her, like an uncontrollable panic attack. This wasn't a Rift to the Netherworld, so where did it lead? She saw David standing to her right in her peripheral vision, and heard the shuffling footsteps of the others behind her.

"You ready?" asked David. Kara noticed a slight waver in his voice.

Kara just nodded. She didn't want David and the others to hear the panic in her voice. She fought to control her composure. The black wall rippled, but Kara saw only the laughing face of a bald archangel.

She clenched her fists—and stepped into the Rift.

CHAPTER 4
LOST SOUL

Kara felt her body being pulled by a powerful source, like a giant vacuum sucking her in. She opened her eyes. Blackness surrounded her. It was like being sucked into space. She couldn't tell what was up or down; it all looked the same to her. Something pulled at her leg, then her arms. Was she going to split apart? She was terrified of drifting in the black abyss until her mind shut off, and she turned into shadow. She feared that jumping into the rift had been a mistake.

Light shone at the edges of her vision, like a light at the end of a tunnel. A setting sun of red and orange appeared before her. With a last tug, Kara was propelled forward towards the light. She fell head first onto a soft surface. She lifted her head. Her hands were covered in a red sticky film of cobwebs and strings. She sat on her knees and shook her hands. It wasn't coming off. Her nostrils burned with the sudden stench of rotten flesh and bile. She wiped her hands on her pants and looked around.

She stood in a cave. A shiver rolled up her back. The walls were covered in folds of decomposing and blackened tissue. Yellow pus-like liquid oozed from what looked like large, infected sores from the walls. Kara watched a piece of flesh peel off and drop to the ground, followed by a crack and a pop. Sheets of meat dripped and slipped to the soft ground in a sticky red carpet. Torches lined the length of the cave on either side, like an underground runway. Kara could see that the cave appeared to go for miles in each direction, with twists and turns as other adjoining tunnels disappeared into shadow. And in the distance, Kara could hear the faint sound of drips that she hoped was water and not something else. The air was hot and heavy, and Kara couldn't wait to get out.

A sucking sound reached her ears. Suddenly, Kara was hit in the chest by a strong force, and she crashed onto the ground. Weight pinned her down. She blinked and looked up into David's smiling face.

"Hey babe. This is a bit fast for a first date — but I don't mind."

"Oh, please!" Kara rolled her eyes, but she couldn't help the smile that reached her lips. David's weight felt awfully good to her, and part of her didn't want him to move. But she didn't want the others to see her in this compromising position.

"Get off me!" She pushed David off of her just in time to see Peter and Jenny crash land beside them in a sticky mess.

"What took you guys so long?" Kara fought with the gooey substance in her hair. She gave up after a while, since the more she pulled, the worse it got.

"This is disgusting! What *is* this place?" Jenny jumped to her feet and looked around. She made a face. "It's like a giant meat grinder. And it smells disgusting."

David picked at the wall with his blade and cut off a piece of decayed tissue. "Figures why Zadkiel would pick this place of all places to hide. He always did smell rotten. He probably feels right at home in this palace of flesh jam."

Kara watched Peter adjusting his glasses. He opened his palm to reveal a small floating red orb.

"Can you read anything in here, Peter?" asked Kara, and she waddled up to him. Her boots sank further into the red mess.

"Can you tell where my mother's soul is? Can you pinpoint a location for it?" She felt her nerves prickle inside of her body. There was no way of knowing if her mother's soul was still intact and unharmed. Zadkiel could have destroyed it long ago, and it pained her to think about it.

Peter's eyes were fixed on the orb for a moment. He moved a trembling hand to face the orb towards the south part of the tunnel. The light dimmed inside the orb, as though controlled by a dimmer. He then brought the orb slowly around in a circle until it shone a little brighter. He looked up. "It's that way. I'm sure of it. I'm picking up faint traces of your mother's soul energy. But I'm picking up something else too. Something's interfering with the readings. But I can't make out what it is. Could be demons — or new breeds."

Kara sighed in relief. Her mother's soul was here, in this horrible meat cave. But there was still the matter of the archangel Zadkiel. She had witnessed his show of power at the council earlier. He wouldn't make it easy for her, she knew, but she would find it nevertheless.

"How long do we have until the Rift closes, Peter?" asked Kara, and she looked at a rippling part of the flesh wall she guessed was the rift's source.

Peter pursed his lips. "About … twenty minutes … maybe more, maybe less."

"Then we don't have much time." David wiped his blade on his jeans and then pointed towards the tunnel. "Just more walls of cooked ham. Nothing to it." He stalked along the walls, his boots making loud suction noises as he pulled them out and pushed them in, again and again.

Kara glanced down the eerie tunnel. The cracks and pops of falling flesh were nauseating. Its sickly red walls made the hairs on the back on her neck stand up. Evil lurked here. She felt it in her being. Kara reached into her jacket and drew out a soul blade. The silver dagger reflected the red from the walls. It looked more like a blood dagger now than a soul one. She brandished it before her.

"We can't underestimate Zadkiel. He was clever enough to fool the council all these years. Who knows what he's capable of? And what he's already done. Stay sharp. There's probably more than this sticky stuff in here. I just want my mother's soul back."

David turned and looked at Kara. "I don't underestimate him. He's still the same bald idiot as before...just that now he prefers to sleep in this five-star meat hotel." A mischievous smile flashed across David's face, lightening Kara's mood.

The group ventured cautiously inside the tunnel. Its sinister walls made Kara feel claustrophobic. With Kara in the lead and Jenny following closely behind her with her bow and arrow at the ready, Peter was sandwiched between them. David held the back. They walked like this for a few minutes, glancing back over their shoulders every now and again. Kara felt uneasy. She noticed the walls seeped more and more of that pus-like liquid. Walking became increasingly difficult. With every step they took, more liquid oozed out of deep gashes, like squeezing the water out of a sponge.

Suddenly, the ground shook.

Clumps of flesh dropped from the ceiling with sickening splashes. Kara steadied herself, her blade held up before her. She heard a distant rumble, like the growl of thunder before a storm. And then it stopped.

"What was that?" whispered Peter, the whites of his eyes gleaming in his petrified face.

Kara met David's concerned expression but didn't answer. She tightened her grip on her soul blade and saw Jenny in the corner of her eye nocking an arrow. Unconsciously, Kara took a step back towards Peter.

A loud growl split the silence. The ground trembled with more intensity, and Kara thought they were in the middle of some sort of quake. But she knew that was impossible. She felt a tightness around her leg. Suddenly, she was thrown across the tunnel. She hit the wall. Her body sank into the soft tissue, as though the walls were made of Jell-O. The decaying stench burned her nose, and Kara's fear escalated. She struggled to move. Her limbs didn't respond. It was as if she was Krazy Glued, pinned against her will. She felt her body being pulled back deeper into the wall. She glanced down and winced. A large red tentacle was wrapped tightly around her legs. Hundreds of open suction cups revealed pointed teeth, like gaping mouths ready to feed. Yellow liquid rolled off the large tentacle.

Someone screamed.

Peter was completely covered by the tentacles. They wrapped around him like a giant boa constrictor crushing its prey before swallowing it whole. She watched him struggle against the creatures and felt instant pity for him. Kara saw a dozen or more tentacles sprout out of the walls and lash at David. With two soul blades in his hands, David slashed and sliced at the creatures. Thumps of severed tentacles littered the floor around him. And soon David was covered in the foul-smelling liquid.

Kara yanked her head to the left. Jenny stabbed a horde of tentacles with her arrow. She punctured one right through its body, and it retreated back into a hole in the wall. Kara watched in horror as a dozen more tentacles shot from what Kara believed were sores, and launched themselves at Jenny. Two grabbed her legs and another two knocked the bow and arrow out of her hands. Jenny tripped and fell face down against the ground. A slippery tentacle advanced towards her face. It whipped out at her; the suction cups stuck to her face. The tentacle radiated from the inside, like a light bulb beneath a shade. Kara heard Jenny's muffled scream and a last suction cup wrapped around her face. The tentacle shuddered and moved, and Kara saw light move inside it, as though it was swallowing. Kara realized in horror that the creature was drinking Jenny's essence. Her eyes flicked over to Peter. He had a suction cup over his face now.

With a tremendous effort, Kara freed her right arm. With her blade still wrapped tightly in her hand, she brought it down and cut through one of the tentacles. It landed with a thud on the ground. Another tentacle came at her from the opposite wall. But she was ready. It flew towards her at great speed, and Kara met it with a side slash. She cut through the flesh easily. Yellow and red liquid sprayed the walls. She felt the ground shake. Twenty more tentacles shot through the walls and came for her. The more she cut, the more tentacles came back.

Frantically, Kara cut through the remaining tendrils around her legs. Chunks of tentacles sprawled around her boots. She looked up. Another tentacle lashed at her. She jumped out of the way and rolled on the ground. She jumped up and was immediately assaulted by another wave of tentacles. Kara ducked, jumped, and sliced her way to her friends. Yellow liquid sprayed her face, and she saw David pull Peter free from the creature's grasp. Peter's essence was seeping through large gaps in his face. His skin was translucent; she could see the brilliant light inside him. His skin was barely holding him together. He looked sick.

David glanced towards Kara. "Help, Jenny!" he yelled over the commotion, as he squished a severed tentacle beneath his boot.

Kara kicked and slashed her way towards her friend. She could hardly see her anymore. The creature had covered Jenny completely in a tangle of red stringy limbs. Frenzied, Kara began to slice pieces off, careful not to cut Jenny. She could see David standing before Peter and doing a good job at cutting the tentacles off of him.

A sharp pain stung the back of Kara's head. She fell forward and reached out. She wrapped her hand around a slippery mass that stuck to her head. It felt strangely like a helmet. She moved her fingers around and touched a suction cup. She shivered. She felt a tingling sensation on the back of her head, like millions of little pricks at the same time. She felt her energy draining away and knew the creature was sucking out her essence. With her blade still clutched in her hand, Kara reached behind her head and stabbed the creature repeatedly. She felt a release and finally pulled the suction cup from her scalp and tossed it. With her strength renewed somewhat, Kara assaulted the creatures again. Chunks of limbs rolled onto the ground like logs. Soon Kara could see Jenny, and with a final effort, she yanked the last meaty tendril from her friend. Jenny collapsed in her arms, her eyes barely open.

Kara shook her gently. "Jenny? Jenny? Can you hear me?"

Jenny's skin was nearly transparent. Kara could see gaping wounds over her entire body. White light spilled through them. It had been a mistake to bring them with her. Jenny's and Peter's wounds were too severe. They had to go back —

The ground trembled...a sucking noise...she turned to see dozens more tentacles sprout from the fleshy walls. Dread rippled through her. How were they going to escape?

"David! We can't stay here. We need to take Peter and Jenny back!"

Kara dropped Jenny to the ground and sliced the head of the nearest tentacle. Another ten tentacles lashed out at her.

And then all at once, the creatures retreated. Like worms wiggling into the ground, the tendrils recoiled back into their fleshy walls.

A man stood at the far end of the tunnel. His red robe billowed around him. The light of the torches reflected off his bald head. Zadkiel! Even in the distance, Kara could see the malevolent smile across his face. He held a small jar in his right hand. And in the jar was a ball of brilliant light.

Zadkiel laughed softly. "You are so predictable, Kara Nightingale. Just like all the others — a mortal-loving blundering fool. I knew you would follow me. I knew you would come for your mother. I've been waiting for you."

Kara was relieved to see the luminance of her mother's soul.

"Give it back. And I'll let you live."

She raised her blade. Her anger had awakened her elemental power. She called it forth, and it answered eagerly. She could feel it opening up inside her like a blooming flower. She saw the fear in the archangel's eyes. He tried to hide it, but she saw it, nonetheless. He wasn't so sure that she couldn't kill him.

Zadkiel's face was a hard mask. "Your mother is a very *ordinary* angel. She has no special talents. I don't know why you risk so much for her — for her miserable soul. It's pathetic really."

Kara lowered her eyes. "I don't care what you think. You're going to give it back."

The archangel leaned forward a little, his broad shoulders hunched. "I don't like *threats*. Especially coming from the mouth of a stupid girl. Besides, you're in no position to make them. Look around you. Your friends are dying. And believe me, they will not last long in the mouth of an ungor demon."

"The mouth of a what?" David looked widely around. He tested his blade against the soft red walls. "We're in the mouth of some demon? Seriously?"

The walls growled as if in answer.

Kara looked over to Jenny and Peter. Their skin was as thin as tracing paper. They were in bad shape. She had to get them out of here.

"Unfortunately for you, the ungor answers to me," said Zadkiel.

Tentacles lashed out, and wrapped themselves around Jenny and Peter. "Make any sudden movements ... and it will kill your precious friends."

Kara stumbled forward. "Let them go! What is it that you want? My mother's soul means nothing to you. My friends mean nothing to you. Where's Asmodeus? Why are you still here?"

"To deliver a message."

His tone was smooth, but Kara detected a hint of deceit. She was sure this was a trick. "What's the message?"

"The Legion must not interfere. They are too late. Mortals are weak, and they do not deserve their world. They are destroying it. It is time to take it back. Besides, it is too late for the Legion. The Legion cannot interfere ... or it will suffer the consequences. I have to thank you, Kara. You were an important piece to my master's plans. Without you, it would not have been possible. Soon we will rule the mortal world."

His words hit Kara hard. "Asmodeus will never rule Earth. The Legion won't allow it."

The corners of Zadkiel's mouth lifted. "But that is not for them to decide, demon spawn. Yes, I call you by your true name, Kara. It's time you stop lying to yourself. Do you really believe that you are a good little angel? You are a demon like your father."

Kara recoiled, terrified that what he said might be true. *No.* It couldn't be true. She was a guardian angel, sworn to protect the mortals. She pushed the doubt out of her mind and scowled at him. "I am not a demon. I'm a guardian angel—"

"Wrong again, demon. Soon you will understand … and you will join us. It is only a matter of time until you figure out which side you're on. My lord asks you to join him now, on his crusade—and he will spare your life."

Kara looked at him hard. "I will never join him. I'd rather die than join a monster. You are trying to destroy the world that I love."

"So be it. You will rot with the rest of them."

"I'm tired of your crap! I'm not listening to this anymore. Give me my mother's soul. Right now! It's two against one, and the odds are in our favor. Give me my mother's soul … or you're going to die."

"That's right, Mrs. Demon—oh, you don't mind that I call you by *your* true name, right?" David stood beside her. "It'll be a pleasure to kick your ass. And a very big one I might add—"

Zadkiel's expression darkened. A smile twitched on his lips. "You were always too outspoken for my taste, David McGowan. Well then, perhaps I too can play this little game." He reached into the jar and pulled out the glowing sphere. "One false move, and I will squish this little soul."

Kara stepped forward, her golden power sizzling on her finger tips. "Don't do anything stupid … if you care about your own stinking soul."

"You want this?" The archangel lifted the soul into the air and gazed at it. He looked at Kara. "Then go get it—"

The little sphere rocketed in the air.

Kara lunged for the soul. In one swift movement, she jumped and caught it. The tiny ball of light illuminated her face and her hands. She held it carefully, as though it might break into pieces in her hands.

Images of different women flickered in her mind's eye. An East Indian woman with long black hair wearing a red and gold sari smiled as she waved her hands around in a dance. Another face; this time it was a weather-beaten woman's face. She was covered in animal furs and sat in the snow sewing wet sealskin onto a kayak frame. She saw an image of her mother as a young girl on roller skates—then as a grown woman holding an infant to her breast. Kara smiled. This was indeed her mother's soul.

"Kara!"

By the time Kara whirled around, Zadkiel was already on the move. She heard him laugh as he dashed down the gullet of the ungor demon. His red robe rippled behind him like a flag caught in a strong wind.

Anger rose inside her. She dropped the soul carefully into her jacket pocket and ran after him.

"Kara! No!"

She heard David's plea, but she couldn't stop. She wouldn't stop. Not until Zadkiel had paid for what he did. She rocketed through the tunnel, her boots churning up the sticky floors. She caught a glimpse of a red robe vanish into another passageway, or was it an alimentary canal leading away from the creature's stomach. Kara quivered at the thought. Either way, she reached it within seconds. She bolted down the food canal and stopped.

Kara found herself in a large rounded area with the same wet red walls. What was different in this space were the wooden desks and chairs that stood at the opposite end. A large bookcase rose to the top. Books spilled from its shelves, ragged and torn. Their leather bonds disintegrated into dust. Kara looked around. This must have been where Zadkiel retreated after a long day's work at the council — to conspire against the Legion, and most probably to communicate with Asmodeus in the safety of the beast's belly.

Zadkiel stood in the center of the cavity. He tilted his head and half smiled, as though taunting Kara to come closer. A black mist rolled up behind him, a rift that wavered like a mirage of water.

"I should have killed you when I had the chance," laughed the archangel softly.

"But you didn't." Kara threw her Soul Blade.

The archangel stepped back into the Rift — and disappeared.

With a soft thud, her blade fell onto the sticky ground.

CHAPTER 5
FALLING TO PIECES

Kara hadn't even let David hold her mother's soul while they helped Jenny and Peter back through the Rift. It is not that she didn't trust him; she just couldn't bring herself to let it go. Kara clutched the soul protectively against her chest, like a mother would her own child. With every little elevator jolt, she found herself tightening her grip. It was as though she had Krazy Glued her hands to the brilliant ball.

Once they were safely back in Horizon and headed towards the Healing-Xpress, Kara said her goodbyes and took off towards the Hall of Souls. David had offered to accompany her, but she brushed him off. She told him that she needed to do this alone. It was her own fault her mother's soul had gone missing in the first place. She could only relax once she knew her mother's soul was safe—finally, and once and for all.

The elevator swayed slightly to the right, then to the left. Kara cupped the soul tenderly. Her eyes never left the operator. An ape with long light brown fur and a small black face, watched her from his chair. His hands and feet were completely black, as though he were wearing gloves. He wore a green tall hat that engulfed his tiny head, as though it was two sizes too big. He looked like an ugly leprechaun. His black beady eyes observed her. His eyes glanced at the soul momentarily. They flashed with sudden interest. Kara pressed her lips into a hard line and hid the soul within her jacket. The ape raised its eyebrows and kept staring at her. She looked him in the eye, stone faced, without blinking. She didn't care that he was supposed to be one of the good guys. If he tried anything, she would cut him up into tiny monkey cubes.

After a few moments, the elevator wrenched to a stop. With a *ding*, the doors slid open. The operator pulled off his hat and bowed.

"Level four! Hall of Souls!" he called, to no one in particular.

Kara pressed the soul protectively against her chest and stepped off the elevator.

She heard the doors close behind her. She looked around. She stood still.

The once brilliantly lit chamber with millions of hovering spheres was now dark and gloomy. Kara's favorite giant field of fireflies had been extinguished. Her chest tightened. Only a few thousand spheres still floated radiantly in the black sky, casting a lonely glow in the vast space. A chill passed through her. What was going on?

Kara gazed at the ground. The black marble floor was covered with dark grey powder, like a plush carpet of dust. Dead souls, Kara realized in horror. Everywhere she looked, dead souls littered the ground. It was like staring at the ashes from the aftermath of a volcanic eruption with mounds of cinders everywhere. The ground was completely covered. There was nowhere for her to walk, if she didn't want to step on the remains of a soul. She bent down and reached out—but pulled her hand back. She cringed as she remembered the feeling of dread and despair she had once felt, while handling a dead soul, Mrs. Wilkins's dead soul. It had been a horrible experience for her, and she never wanted to feel it again. But something told her that this was an entirely different situation.

A shiver passed through her. She could see a huge stone fireplace in the distance. She remembered the magnificent white flames that sprouted high into the air. But there weren't any flames now. The white fires of Atma were doused. Dread crept inside her like a fever. She forced the frightening feeling aside and thought of the archangel Ramiel. He would explain this to her.

Kara stuck out her leg, and gently tapped one of the dead souls—nothing happened. Curious, she pushed it to the side with her boot. She still felt nothing. There were no intense feelings of despair and misery. No voices screamed inside her head. No visions of past lives fluttered inside her mind's eye. It was as though it had never happened. She tapped it again, and the soul rolled over and stopped—like a black ball, hollow and dead. What had happened to the soul? Why it wasn't crying out when she touched it, she couldn't tell. Something was terribly wrong.

Kara made her way carefully through the thousands of dead souls that littered the ground, brushing them gently with her boots, so as not to step on them. God forbid if she stepped on one of them. Her footsteps echoed throughout the chamber, a strange and lonely sound in the majestic space. She strained her eyes to see beyond the peppered black sky. The room was still, nothing moved. It felt dead to Kara. She looked for the blond haired children, but she couldn't see any. Where were the cherubs?

Crunch.

Kara frowned and glanced at the floor. She stood in a small mound of sparkling sand, as though someone had dumped a pile of diamonds on the ground. She brushed her boot through it. How beautiful the stones looked against the black marble floor. Her mother loved diamonds. But they could never afford to buy the real ones, only the zirconia. She tapped the soul gently against her chest.

"I'll buy you real diamonds one day, mom. I promise."

A sparkle caught her eye a few feet away. More piles of diamonds, she realized. And now that she knew what to look for, she noticed hundreds more hidden beneath the blackened souls. Strange. She had never noticed them before.

A scraping sound reached her ears. She whirled around — and a golden haired person with long blue robes fell into her arms. Balancing the cherub with one arm, Kara slowly lowered herself to the ground. He was surprisingly light. She positioned herself on her knees and brought the little child closer to her—and froze.

An emaciated face with sunken eyes with a nose and mouth lost in hundreds of wrinkles looked up at her. His withered skin was like parchment and stretched over his skull-like face; it looked as though it would disappear. This was not the youthful face of the cherubs she remembered. She was staring at the face of an ancient man. His lips moved, but no sound escaped his mouth. Kara felt him shivering in her arms. Gaunt grey feet stuck out from beneath his blue robes, like a cadaver from the morgue. Kara desperately tried to wrap his robe around him. She thought of crying out for help, but thought better of it. She felt as though he would break if she raised her voice. She brushed his thin hair from his face with shaking fingers. His lips moved again. She lowered her ear near his lips.

"Save us."

Kara felt suddenly cold. She frowned. "What? What do you mean … save us? What's wrong with you?"

The cherub's eyes rolled back in his head. He didn't answer.

Kara fidgeted uncomfortably. "I'm … I'm going to lift you up now—and take you to Raphael. Just hang on."

Delicately, Kara balanced the cherub tenderly against the left side of her chest. She remembered having dolls heavier than he was. It frightened her. She glanced down at her mother's soul, still clutched gently to her chest, and was careful not to squish it with the cherub's weight. She knew that was probably unlikely, since the little guy weighed no more than her neighbor's cat.

"Save us … you must save us," croaked the cherub again, and Kara noticed how much louder the voice was, as though he had gained some strength back.

She stopped and looked gently at him. "I'm going to get you some help. Don't you worry. Don't talk … save your strength."

The cherub lifted his hand and pressed a finger against Kara's forehead. She shivered as his touch sent a cold chill from her head down to her toes, as though someone had poured a bucket of ice-cold water on her head. A sudden burst of emotions exploded inside her. Voices screamed inside her head. Millions of people cried out to her at the same time. She could hear them clearly, as though they were right there beside her. Her vision blurred. She blinked. Images of different men, women, and children flashed in her mind's eye, like a fast-forwarding movie. More like a dream, she realized. All at once, she felt their joy and their pain. A man walked his dog in a lush green park. A middle-aged woman with a straw hat worked feverously in her garden. Children laughed and chased each other on a playground. A black mist approached. The children screamed. Shadows swallowed the children and muffled their screams. Darkness came. She heard the screams of thousands of mortals. She heard their pleas for help. Creatures from their nightmares tore at their bodies, ripping them limb from limb.

Kara cried out, just as the people in her mind cried out as they died —

The visions disappeared.

Kara trembled and looked down into the wet golden eyes of the cherub. His mouth opened in a soundless cry. Suddenly, his skin and robe began to glow. They shone brilliantly like crystals. The skin cracked. Kara noticed small crevices forming on the cherub's face, like a puzzle. And with a sudden pop, the cherub exploded in a cloud of diamonds.

"No!"

Terrified, Kara searched the air in front of her with her hands trying desperately to catch some of the falling particles. She watched them drift to the ground. The cherub was now a beautiful pile of glimmering diamonds.

Kara fell to her knees. She grabbed a fistful of the tiny crystals and watched them fall through her fingers like grains of salt. Overcome with sadness, Kara cursed the fact that she couldn't cry.

"They are dying," said a voice behind her.

Kara whipped around and stared up into the face of a giant man. He was dressed in a white robe, open in the front with a high gold-rimmed collar and gold rimmed cuffs. His handsome face was twisted in grief. A golden glow emanated from his pale skin.

"There is nothing we can do," said the archangel Ramiel solemnly.

"He — he just exploded into dust in my arms!" Kara lifted her arms dramatically in the air. "What is happening to them?"

The archangel's lips were a hard line. "The cherubs ... are all dying." He gestured before them.

Kara followed his gaze and cringed. About half a dozen cherubs, their faces skeletal and sickly, strained to walk. They teetered to and fro, unable to keep their balance. The agony on their faces pained Kara. She pitied them.

A cherub shuffled towards them. Hunched over, as though his back was broken, he could barely walk. His shrunken face was lifeless and his eyes were a milky white like a blind man's. And with a final effort, the cherub fell forward and landed head first on the ground. Within seconds his body exploded in a cloud of brilliant particles. All that remained was a small pyramid of diamonds. She stared in horror at the hundreds of piles of cherub dust. The ground was covered in these mounds.

Kara studied Ramiel for a moment. "But, why are they dying? How *can* they die? I thought the cherubs were immortal?"

Ramiel bent down to examine the remains of a cherub. "Cherubs exist as long as souls exist. Without souls, the cherubs will die. They need the life force of the souls to live."

Unconsciously, Kara hugged the soul inside her jacket and stared up into the black sky. Only a few thousand of souls hovered above and around them. It was like staring up into the sky at night, trying to see the stars though the clouds. She set her jaw and squinted at the ground. Millions of dead souls covered the floor. She feared the worse. The cherub's last words echoed in her ears.

Save us.

A cry escaped her lips. She was responsible. She knew that she had enabled thousands of demons to enter the mortal world. Thousands of souls lay dead because of her. "The demons are killing the souls," said Kara.

"Yes," answered Ramiel. "It is a savage attack. Brutality on a colossal magnitude against the mortal world. We have never been faced with such an atrocity before. The death toll of souls has reached unfathomed proportions."

"What will happen to the rest of the cherubs?" Kara's chest tightened. She watched the little figures dragging themselves around the chamber. She reached into her jacket pocket. "There are still souls that live. They're not all dead — here. This is my mom's. Keep her safe." Kara handed her mother's glowing white sphere to the archangel.

Ramiel took the soul carefully and studied it. He looked up at Kara suddenly, with a perplexed expression. "How did you get it back? I thought Zadkiel had destroyed it —"

Kara sighed. "Long story ... but I got her back."

The archangel looked at Kara thoughtfully. "Well, she will be safe here —"

"Kara!"

Kara turned to see David jogging towards them. His face was drawn and tight. He gave Ramiel a nod, and Kara found it strange that he didn't insult the archangel as he usually did.

"David, what's wrong?" asked Kara, and she started to feel nervous again.

"All the guardians are being called to an emergency meeting," said David as he jammed his hands in his front pockets, "… on Lieutenant Michael's orders. We're meeting at Operations."

"What's the meeting about?" Kara suspected that the dying souls and cherubs were part of it.

"No idea. But I know it's big … something's going down for sure. I've never seen a meeting of this magnitude."

Kara didn't like the sound of that. She felt responsible. She had been a pawn in Asmodeus's plan. Without her, the Mirror of Souls wouldn't have worked, and the demons couldn't have entered the mortal world. She was like Asmodeus — an abomination to the angel world, a half-breed, bred only for one purpose — to destroy the mortal world. She clenched her jaw. She would get her revenge. *You are not my father.* She made a silent promise to herself that she would do everything in her power to mend the horrors she had unleashed. And then it would be payback time.

"When do we leave?" asked Kara, her voice deep and trembling with rage. She remembered Asmodeus's joyful face as his demons slipped into the mortal world and began tearing their way through human hearts.

David raised his brows. "Right now."

CHAPTER 6
THE LEGION OF ANGELS

Kara followed David down the red dunes. The sun beat down on her head, and Kara felt as if she had a hot hairdryer close to the scalp. She watched David's back, but she wasn't really watching him. She couldn't stop thinking about the cherub who had died in her arms. His withered face haunted her, like a bad dream that lingered after she had opened her eyes.

Save us, the cherub had said. What did he mean by that? And why did he tell her? Was she supposed to do something? Was she part of a bigger plan? She didn't know. And she couldn't shut her mind up about it.

A loud rumbling reached her ears. Kara looked over the brow of the dune she was climbing — and stopped dead in her tracks.

Hundreds of thousands of guardian angels filled the entire valley below her, a moving sea of angels readying for battle. They gathered together and formed straight lines down and across the valley, a perfect square, a full strength angel Legion. Kara's body prickled in excitement. She had never seen so many guardians together in one area. She felt small and insignificant.

A sense of pride welled in her chest. She felt intoxicated. She wanted to run amongst them, to stand amongst them all. With an army like this, anything was possible.

She smelled iron and salt water. The crowd seemed to disperse as she and David made their way through it. Did the Legion still believe her to be a traitor? She could hear whispers from the crowd. Anxious faces surrounded her. They were nervous, like caged animals. Kara tensed.

A sparkle at the head of the Legion caught her attention. Kara looked over the heads of the crowds. A giant man made his way across the front lines. Yards of silver cloth rippled in the wind behind him like a flag made of pixie dust. Even in the distance, she recognized the archangel Michael. His golden brown skin shone brightly in the sunlight. His silky dark brown hair brushed his muscular shoulders, and his hands were clasped into fists.

She felt a tug on her arm and turned to see David beckoning her to follow him. He pulled her towards a small mount of sand. Kara climbed closely behind him. Once they reached the top, she looked over the thousands of heads and focused on Michael. He stood with his hands clasped in front of him, his body hard and stiff like a Greek statue.

"Guardians," boomed Michael's voice across the desert. His voice was magically enhanced and all the guardians could hear him as clearly as though he were right in front of each of them.

"We are gathered here in this late hour to *inform* you and to *prepare* you all for what lies ahead. As some of you have already heard, thousands of portals have been opened, and hundreds of thousands of demons have been released into the mortal world. The legion has never faced a threat of this magnitude before. Innocent men, women, and children have been attacked in their own homes and ripped into pieces."

Whispers spread through the crowd like a wildfire. Kara lowered her head. Was Michael blaming her? She heard a hint of an accusation in his words. Her throat tightened as she fought to control her emotions. She remembered hearing the cries of children as the demons tore out their hearts. This was all her fault.

Something brushed against her fingers. She felt a hand interlace with hers. She looked up and met David's concerned face. His blue eyes glistened. He gave her hand a reassuring squeeze. She squeezed back. She never wanted him to let go.

She wished silently that she could get away from all of this— that she and David could be together somehow back on Earth, away from the horrors and the atrocities that seemed likely to come to pass. But she knew she could never have the romantic life she had always envisioned with the man she loved. She was a guardian angel sworn to protect the humans. The mortal world was in turmoil. They needed to be saved. And Kara had a job to do.

She lifted her gaze back to Michael, but not before she caught the disapproving glances from a few angels. Their faces appeared to be twisted in disgust as they looked from David to Kara. She forced herself to look away.

"Thousands of souls are dying each day," continued Michael. "Each second we waste here, is another dead soul. We have all sworn to protect them. We are the chosen ones. It is our mandate to save the mortal souls.

"As of this moment—all previous assignments are cancelled. Angels, you have but one assignment. To rid the mortal world of demons!"

His last word echoed throughout the vast dunes like thunder. Angels jumped into the air and roared like a giant wave that rose and spread through the crowd. It was both incredible and terrifying at the same time.

Michael lifted his arms into the air and called for silence. He waited for the crowd to quiet before he continued. "Asmodeus believes that he has won. But he is seriously mistaken. And we will show him. We will strike at the demon lord's heart! Our legions will *crush* his armies, and we will give Earth back to its rightful inhabitants!" He raised his fist. "This will be the biggest battle this Legion has ever fought. The battle has just begun! And we will be victorious!"

An explosion of roars erupted all around. Angels jumped up and batted the air with their fists. Kara stared into maddened faces. She could practically see the venom dripping from their mouths. It was hatred—hatred for the demons. The angels wanted to destroy Asmodeus and his demons just as badly as she did.

A sudden loud crunching sound echoed around them. The crowds below them separated, and a mass of more than a hundred oracles rolled themselves towards Michael. Their silver gowns and long white beards flowed behind them. The sun's rays flickered within their giant crystal balls, forcing Kara to shield her eyes. They reached the archangel and formed two rows on either side of him. The oracles waited patiently above their crystals.

Michael regarded the oracles for a moment, before turning and addressing the guardians.

"Guardians. Hear me now. If the entire human race is annihilated, there will be no more souls to protect, and we will have no reason to exist. We must save the mortals to guarantee our own survival. If we cannot rid the mortal world of Asmodeus's armies … we will cease to exist."

Kara saw horror spreading across the guardians' faces. It was a falsehood, a half-truth that angels were immortal. Kara had seen death with her own eyes—she knew that angels could die.

For a long moment, the vast desert was silent.

Michael spoke at last. "All guardians will be paired into groups of fifty and assigned to specific cities or towns around the world. The Counter Demon Division will remain intact and will be responsible to track down Asmodeus and seize him. Our Scouts have pinpointed several possible locations. We will bring the demon lord to justice. And he will be executed!"

Kara flinched as a deafening roar erupted all around her. Images of Jenny and Peter flashed in her mind's eye. She missed her friends. She felt a sting at her core that she wasn't part of CDD anymore. It had been an exciting post. They needed her — her powers could help them. The CDD had no idea how strong Asmodeus really was.

Michael surveyed the crowd for a moment. Even in the distance, Kara could see the unmistakable strain upon his face.

"I will not lie to you and tell you that this will be an easy battle. Many of you will perish. But hear me now. Do not let that stop you. We are soldiers first, and then angels. We will answer our Legion's call and fight. Fight till the end! We must protect the mortals at whatever cost. It is time, Guardians. May Horizon protect you! Oracles...

Kara watched as the oracles rolled their giant crystal balls back down the red dunes towards the pools. Their long white beards trailed behind them. The desert rumbled as the host of guardians followed behind them. The sand vibrated below Kara's feet.

Before long the crowd around her dispersed, and Kara spotted a group of CDD guardians walking towards the elevator.

"Kara!"

Jenny jogged up the rise. Her purple hair sparkled in the sun. Her eyes were wide with excitement. She was holding a small black leather case. She held it up to Kara.

"Here — you've been reinstated to CDD."

Kara reached out and took the case. As soon as she flipped it open, she recognized the golden key card secured on the inside. Without the golden key she couldn't reach level five, the best kept secret in Horizon — the Department of Defense.

Kara pulled out the golden key and turned it over in her hand. "I never thought they'd let me back in ... after everything that's happened." She struggled to control her emotions.

Jenny's eyes gleamed. "Well they are letting you back in. Cassiel asked for you personally — said the team wasn't complete without Kara. He wants you back, girl."

"Really?"

"Yup." Jenny pulled on the ends of her purple hair and twirled them around her fingers. "It's crazy in there. The entire unit is going mental."

"It's not just *your* unit that's going mental," said David. He watched the hoards of guardians intensely. "I've never seen the Legion so agitated. I can see the fear in their eyes. They're afraid of what's out there. They're afraid to die — a true death."

Kara could see the fear spreading across some of their faces. "They should be afraid. They're not just saving mortal lives from some freak accident anymore. They have to fight against demons." She bit her lower lip and spoke softly. "The new breeds are going to tear them apart."

David's handsome face crumpled into an ugly look of concern. His mouth was a hard line. Kara wanted to reach out to him.

"Well, it's definitely bad." Jenny's eyes were filled with worry. She sighed. "We should get going."

Kara struggled to restrain herself from grabbing David's hand. She didn't want him to fight without her. The thought of losing David was unimaginable. She didn't think she could go on if something were to happen to him.

He seemed to be thinking the same thing. "I don't like it," he said finally.

"What?"

He turned to Kara. "That you're going back to CDD. The unit's been breached. You remember what happened with those douche bags. You can't trust anyone."

Kara gave David a reassuring smile. "I know. I'm sure Cassiel is aware of it also. He won't let anything happen to me. Don't worry. I'll be fine. It's *you* I'm worried about."

David's blue eyes sparkled. His lips curled into a smile, and he pressed his hands to his chest. "I knew you loved me — ouch!"

Kara punched him on the arm. "Be serious for once! This isn't a joke. You're always getting into trouble, David. Just ... be careful, okay?" She couldn't believe how lightly he thought of himself. It made her furious.

David lifted his arms in protest. "Okay … okay. Don't worry, I can take care of myself." He pulled a soul blade from inside his jacket. With his hand wrapped around the handle, he raised the blade in the air and examined it closely. The blade glistened in the sun. "I've been waiting for a chance to practice my moves on a few of those new breeds. I'm telling you … they'll be running the other way when they see me coming."

Kara rolled her eyes. "David. Promise me you won't do anything stupid. Promise me."

David grinned. "Me? Do anything stupid? Of course not, cutie—I'm the most responsible, most law-abiding angel in all Horizon."

Even with all the theatrics, Kara knew David well enough to know that he was hiding his true feelings. He was terrified, just as she was. The more he fooled around, the more anxious he truly was. And that only made Kara more nervous.

"See you guys later." And with that, David trotted down the slope and joined the mass of guardians heading for the pools.

Regretfully, Kara watched David disappear under a wave of angels. She clenched her fists as she remembered the half-breed demon who had sucked the life source from her rookie Tom so easily. She knew many angels would die today, probably thousands. *Would these faces make it back? How many angels had the necessary skills to fight higher demons?*

Kara flinched as she remembered the sounds of terrified children screaming and the hungry cries of the demons. She was to blame. She was responsible.

"Come on, Kara." Jenny tugged on her shirt and urged her along. As she galloped down the slope, puffs of red dust flew up behind her like a cape.

Reluctantly, Kara followed Jenny towards the elevators. She could only hope that CDD would be the answer to Asmodeus and his demons — but something in Michael's manner earlier told her that it wouldn't.

CHAPTER 7
TEAMMATES

Kara shoved her CDD case in her front pocket and followed Jenny through a maze of cubicles and chairs. All around them, the Counter Demon Division was alive with sounds. Kara remembered the division being a pretty hectic environment, but this was more like anarchy. Papers fell from the levels above and covered the floors in a white carpet. Angels shouted at each other from across the chamber. They pushed and shoved one another. Some ran around the room, jumping over chairs and desks like deer. Their eyes were filled with panic. They were not the confident faces Kara had seen before.

Screams pierced the cacophony of level five, and Kara could not help but watch the large holographic screens that were mounted in the center of the chamber and along the walls. Every screen showed images of terrified men, women and children. They screamed at the top of their lungs as four-legged demons, with raw-red bodies plagued with oozing sores, ripped easily through the mortals' flesh with their sharp black talons. Blood spurted onto the walls of the rooms on the screens.

Kara heard another scream. It was coming from the holographic screen right in front of her. A young girl with dark brown hair and large brown eyes cowered against a wall. Blood trickled down her petrified face from a large gash on the side of her head. A shiver rolled up Kara's back. The girl looked like a younger version of herself. Something dark flashed across the screen. Kara wanted to warn the girl, but she stood transfixed. A moment later, a shadow demon materialized, grabbed the young girl by the neck and ripped out her heart. Kara forced herself to look away.

She tried to focus on the task at hand, but the screams overpowered her thoughts. Death stared back at her from every screen, a reminder of her failure. A reminder of what she had done.

"You coming?" Jenny appeared beside her and knocked Kara out of her trance. Jenny looked at the screens and then at Kara, "We can't do anything for them now. I know it's hard not look … or not to feel anything — but we have to stay focused." She pressed her hand gently on Kara's shoulder. "Come. We should go."

Kara lowered her eyes. "This is my fault, Jenny," she whispered, keeping her eyes low. "All of it. They're all dying because of me." Her bottom lip trembled.

"You couldn't have known what he intended to do with you, Kara," said Jenny gently. "You can't blame yourself. It wasn't your fault."

A wail came from one of the monitors. Kara flinched. She didn't dare look at the screen. "Without me, this would never have happened. The portals were opened . . . with the mirrors and me ... with my powers. I'm partly responsible. I was part of it."

"Kara—look at me. You can't blame yourself for a madman's plan. You're a good person. You would never have wished this on anyone. You're not a killer. You're a guardian angel." Jenny's green eyes pierced Kara. "We *will* make this right. I promise."

Kara only nodded.

"Come. Let's go." Jenny grabbed Kara's hand and pulled her along.

Half-heartedly, Kara followed Jenny through a mess of desks and chairs to the center of the round chamber. The archangel Cassiel sat at a great table surrounded by a few dozen guardians in black uniforms. His light brown hair was as disheveled as Kara had remembered. He wore black cargo pants and a tight black t-shirt over his muscular chest. He fixed his hazel eyes upon her. It made her uncomfortable. She recognized Peter's petrified face. He gave her a smile, and pushed his glasses up his nose with a trembling finger. She looked away from him and flinched.

Al and Devon sat at the table.

A snicker curled on Devon's lips. His dark eyes sent a chill through Kara. Both boys had hair the color of ravens, but Devon's had a bluish tint to it, making it stand out. His hawk-like nose was the center of his sharp features. He regarded her like prey. She strained to remain calm. She wouldn't let them see her distress. Her eyes moved to Al. His pale skin looked sickly in the light. His black eyes were half-hidden beneath massive eyebrows. She remembered the beam of golden light that had blasted from her hands uncontrollably and struck him in the chest. Although she had gone to prison for her lack of control, she still did not trust him. She had seen the death blade in his hand. There was no mistake in that. He had intended to use it against David, and she wouldn't let that happen.

Al's face betrayed no emotions. Like a mask made of clay, it was dead and fixed upon her. She knew things were going to get ugly. How...she couldn't tell, but she couldn't suppress the nasty feeling that welled inside her.

Cassiel pushed back his chair and stood up. "Ah! At last, Kara! Back amongst us, where you belong." His face beamed, and he made his way towards her. He threw his arms out and embraced her. "Welcome. Welcome back Kara."

Kara made a face because her head was shoved into his armpit. The giant man released her finally and motioned for her and Jenny to sit at the great table.

With his arms clasped behind his back, Cassiel took a turn around the table and settled behind Kara's chair. "The CDD has been given the mandate to seek out the demon lord. We must locate his command center—we know he's there. We must pinpoint its location. We must seek him out."

Seek him out, repeated Kara in her head. She knew it wasn't going to be easy. The demon lord was no ordinary demon — and no fool. He is the king of the Netherworld, their prince of darkness. Kara wasn't sure they could pull it off. How do you kill an archangel, especially one who doesn't want to be found?

Kara felt pressure as Cassiel placed his hands on the backrest of her chair. The chair moved a few inches.

"A single guardian cannot vanquish the demon lord," Cassiel instructed them. "So I don't want anyone trying anything stupid. He is too powerful. He would crush you like a peanut. Listen up! If one team discovers the whereabouts of the demon lord, they will report back to CDD immediately. You will not try and take on the demon lord yourselves. Are we clear? No one is to approach him!"

Kara was thrown forward a little as her chair jerked.

"Your orders are to seek out the command center and report back — with a confirmation of his location. As soon as his identity is confirmed, I will make the necessary calls and wait for further instructions. It is imperative that we succeed. We can't afford any mistakes."

Kara felt pressure against her chair again, as though Cassiel had put his entire weight upon it. She looked up and all eyes were on her. Immediately she stared at the table.

"Again. I don't want anyone trying to be a hero. You got that? Good. Now each team will be given a specific address. We know of five probable locations. You are to scout out the locations, and try to get a positive identification of the demon lord — if he's there. Remember what I said, no one is to strike. You must wait my instructions. Teams are as follows."

Hatred welled inside Kara. She picked at the table, half listening, as Cassiel called out the names of the first teams. She wasn't sure she could just sit tight and wait for backup if she spotted Asmodeus. After what he had done to her, she wanted him to pay. She wanted to hurt him like he hurt her. It was payback time.

A commotion shook her out of her reverie. She thought she heard her name called. She looked up. Everyone was staring at her. What had she missed? She looked from Peter to Jenny — their eyes were filled with distress. Jenny gave Kara a slight shake of her head.

Kara mouthed the word, *what?* But Jenny's eyes were glued above Kara.

"So there you have it, guardians," Kara heard Cassiel say above her head. "Get to it!"

At once, the field agents took to their feet and joined their teams. The sounds of heavy boots scurrying away erupted all around them. Kara took the opportunity to run over to Jenny and Peter.

"What? What's going on? I was in my head … what did I miss?"

Peter and Jenny exchanged a worried look. Jenny took a step towards Kara and whispered to her. "You're teamed with Al and Devon."

"What!" Kara was outraged. She looked over to them. Both Al and Devon were leaning against their chairs, staring back at her. Evil grins spread on their primal faces. They enjoyed seeing her squirm, she realized. She turned quickly away. How could Cassiel put her with these traitors? They had tried to kill David. She hated them. And she was certain they hated her too. She was sure they would try to hurt her again.

"How can Cassiel do this to me? What is wrong with him?"

Jenny closed her eyes for a moment. "That's just it, Kara. I don't get it. And get this — Cassiel paired himself with you, too! He's going on a field mission with you. It's just plain weird, if you ask me."

Peter stuck his head between the two girls. "Maybe he wants to keep an eye on them. See if they'll try anything with you around. He's a big guy … I'm sure he can handle those two idiots. Maybe he's looking for something to pin on them — to prove that they're traitors."

Kara remembered how excited Cassiel had been at the prospect of her using her powers. When the fight had begun between Devon, Al and David, Cassiel had urged her to focus on her anger, to let the elemental power flow. She visualized the stupid grin on his face. "I think he wants to see me use my powers again … like to train me on the battle field or something like that."

"You think?" asked Jenny.

"I don't know. It's possible. He was a little too eager to see me work it before. Maybe he still expects me to be able to do great things." Kara wasn't sure what to believe. Maybe she should have stayed with David. It seemed the lesser of two evils. But something didn't fit. "Have you guys ever been on a mission with Cassiel?"

Jenny looked over her shoulder, making sure no one was listening. "Since I joined CDD, Cassiel has never once gone on field missions … never. And now he's going with them! And you! It doesn't feel right."

Kara knew Jenny was right. Something was definitely wrong. She turned her head and watched as Cassiel clapped Al happily on the back, as though they were old friends reminiscing about old times. Kara felt disgusted.

The archangel raised a large arm in the air. "Kara! Let's go!" He waved at her excitedly, his face beamed.

Kara exchanged a nervous look with Peter and Jenny before treading towards her new team. Cassiel was a little too happy and too eager. While the rest of the angel world was distressed, Cassiel appeared to be ecstatic. How could he be happy, when the mortal world was crumbling.

After replenishing her weapons, Kara followed her new teammates to the vega tanks. She kept a safe distance from them, not wanting to get too close. Every fiber of her being screamed that something was not right. Her three new teammates walked in front of her. Cassiel glanced back, with an innocent smile painted on his face. It made Kara cringe.

They made their way towards a raised platform, where the vega tanks awaited them. The four cubicles of water shimmered like giant emeralds as the light from the ceiling hit the tanks.

Kara watched in silence as the other teams stepped into the tanks one by one. Their bodies in turn disintegrated into sparkling specks of sand, and then disappeared as though they had never been there. She watched Jenny and Peter wave their goodbyes. Soon, Kara and her team were the only ones left.

"Are you ready, Kara?" Cassiel stepped up onto the metal platform, and wedged himself between two tanks. Al and Devon took their places behind him.

Kara made fists with her hands. Against her better judgment, she stepped onto the platform. She felt eyes on her and glanced to her right. An evil grin materialized on Al's face. His dark eyes threatened her. She wished she could throw up.

"We're off to an abandoned psych ward in the small town of Hudson in upstate New York. The scouts believe one of the command centers is there. Keep close." Cassiel grinned widely again, and Kara thought he seemed way too excited for such a serious mission.

"See you on the other side in a few seconds, Kara." And with that, Cassiel walked into the tank. His body exploded in brilliant particles, and then vanished. Al and Devon followed his example.

Kara frowned. Why was Cassiel so happy? And why had he decided to accompany them on this mission? She knew the only way to find out.

She stepped into the wall of green waters.

Chapter 8
St. John's Asylum, NY

Kara walked along a dirt road. Her boots crunched the gravel as she strode up a path that curved up a hill. She felt amazing in her M-suit, despite the fact that she was on a mission with her two arch enemies, Al and Devon. Her M-suit made her feel somewhat invincible, like a superhero.

Rain pattered the top of Kara's head. A soft wind brought with it the smell of wet earth and leaves. It was early spring. Clumps of snow still covered the ground in places, refusing to melt. Squirrels, opposed to the group trespassing on their land, chattered loudly and jumped from the branches of a large evergreen tree. The evening sky was a mixture of browns and blacks, not exactly pretty. The M-5 series suits gave everything an ugly and depressing green tint to it, increasing the tension of their gloomy mission.

Kara had read about this asylum online. It was the most haunting in the entire state. She wondered if ghosts really existed. She had learnt firsthand that angels existed, and demons. Why not ghosts? She shook off a chill, and imagined the sky as a warm orange color.

Distant screams echoed from the town below. Kara stopped abruptly and turned around. The little town was covered in a cloak of darkness. No street lights shone. No house lights. There was no electricity anywhere. Shapes moved in the darkness. Some moved swiftly from door to door, while others glided slowly along the streets, like black specters. A wail pierced the night air. Kara shivered. She recognized the voice of a girl crying out for help — demons. Kara realized in horror that they were attacking the town. She felt her insides tighten. The scream was close. She could help. Involuntarily, she took a step forward —

Something strong caught her arm.

"Going somewhere?"

Kara met Al's glare. He looked wild. His jaw tightened, and he leaned down towards hers.

She shook off his arm. "Don't touch me," she growled, and stood her ground. She squared her shoulders. She wasn't about to let Al intimidate her, even if he was nearly twice her size.

"What's going on here?" Cassiel pushed his way between the two of them. His giant body towered easily over them. He studied their faces. He repeated his question again, annoyed. "I said ... what's going on?"

Since Al wasn't about to say anything, Kara pointed to the town. "That town's in trouble. Demons are attacking the mortals. They're defenseless against these demons. We need to help them."

Cassiel looked over the town in silence. His hazel eyes shimmered in the night light. His face bore no expression. "There's nothing we can do for them now. We can't stray from our mission."

Kara was outraged. "But we can't just leave them there! They're all going to die if we don't help them! There are children down there. Innocent children!"

Devon and Al exchanged an amused look. Kara's rage flared. Innocent children were dying and these two were laughing about it, as if it was some good joke. It was obvious whose side they were on. Why couldn't Cassiel see it too?

"I understand your feelings ... but it's not our mission," said Cassiel, after a moment.

"But we're guardian angels! We're supposed to save them! We swore an oath. We must help them!" Kara threw her arms in the air in a fury.

"Sometimes for the greater good, a few innocent lives will be lost, in order to save millions. We can't save them all, Kara. But we must find the demon lord. That is *our* mandate. He is the cause of all this suffering. We must put an end to it. And to do exactly that ... we must find him first, before he can continue to hurt the mortals."

Kara shrugged. Part of what Cassiel said made sense. But she was sure they could save some lives and still come back to look for Asmodeus. This whole thing smelled rotten.

Cassiel shook his head. "Let's go. We've already wasted too much time." He walked away purposely. Devon and Al followed, but not before they both gave Kara menacing looks.

Kara was left alone. She gazed out on the little town. It had become quiet again. Kara strained for the sound of the girl's screams again. But they didn't come. The town lay silent against the night sky. Nothing moved, not even a shadow. It was a ghost town — now that the demons had killed everyone. Was this what would become of the entire world if they failed?

While Kara ached at the wrongness of it all, she forced herself to follow the others. A mammoth red brick building appeared on the top of the rise. It stood tall and decrepit, like an abandoned castle from another land. Rows of windows decorated the front and sides of the building. A heavy fog covered the tall grasses of the grounds in a thick blanket. There was no forking in the path. The dirt road led them directly to the abandoned building, like an invitation.

Keeping her distance, Kara followed Cassiel and the others up the hill and to the front of the massive structure. They stopped before two majestic wood doors. Cracked red paint and graffiti covered the doors and the front wall. A large padlock held the doors closed securely. Devon pulled out a blade and cut through the metal as easily as if it were butter. He pulled open the doors. A loud screeching sound cut through the night air as the doors swung on their hinges. Kara could make out a dark entry way and a decrepit hallway that opened up to other passageways that were lost in shadow. A thick mildew smell mixed with rot permeated the air around them. The hairs on the back of her neck pricked up. It had a sinister feel about it — the perfect fortress for a fallen angel.

Devon turned and smiled at Kara. He stepped to the side and gestured with his arm. "Ladies first."

Kara shifted her weight uncomfortably. This felt all wrong. She turned to Cassiel. "We can't just barge in here. This place is huge. It's perfect for demons to hide. How do we know even where to look? I suggest we make a plan so we don't get lost in here."

Devon looked smug. "I'm sensing fear." he said. "How can the great Kara Nightingale be frightened of a little adventure? You're not afraid of the dark, are you? Surely with your kind of power, the demon lord doesn't frighten you?"

Cassiel laughed softly, and Kara was reminded of another archangel, with white skin and black hair. No. Cassiel was good. He wouldn't put her in any danger. But why were they with Al and Devon? Clearly he must know about their traitorous intentions? She tried to convince herself that he was just really naïve. It didn't work.

"Well, then. I'll go first." Cassiel drew a moonstone from his jacket pocket. Immediately, the stone shone a brilliant white light, giving off enough light for Kara to see where they were heading.

Kara pulled out a soul blade and followed the archangel inside the great doors. She felt the presence of Al and Devon closely behind her. She forced herself to stay calm.

The rotten smell was a hundred times worse inside. Black mold covered the walls and pieces of tile and metal peeled from the walls and the ceiling, leaving large gaps that oozed an orange liquid. It was as though the entire building was infected with a flesh eating disease. Parts of walls lay crumbled into white piles of plaster, as if a bomb had gone off inside. Orange water dripped from long neglected pipes that ran the length of the hall. Kara thought about reaching out and touching the liquid, but decided against it. The rot smell seemed to be coming from the orange water.

The hall opened up onto a lobby with several doors and hallways branching out. Pieces of broken glass and smashed furniture were scattered on the floor. An old television in a wooden case stood in the far corner on top of crumpled newspapers. Kara wondered what this place had looked like fifty years ago, with nurses in white uniforms helping patients to their rooms. She imagined halls with beautiful white and orange walls and shiny tiled vinyl floors. It must have been beautiful once. But that was a long time ago.

Cassiel pulled out blueprints and studied them for a moment. "Okay, guardians. We're going to split into two teams. The first team will go through that door and down to the basement level." He pointed to an area on the blueprints. Kara stepped closer for a better look. "The other team will go through this door to the left and up two floors. We think he's either hiding in the labs, or in the morgue."

"There's a morgue in this building?" Kara pictured grey rotten corpses lying on metal beds.

"Not anymore," said Cassiel. "We'll meet up back at this lobby in an hour. Al, you're with me. Devon and Kara — you two take the basement. Stay out of sight." He folded the map and shoved it back inside his jacket.

Just her luck, Kara thought. She would have preferred to have been paired with Cassiel. She watched as the archangel and Al disappeared behind a door. His moonstone lighted up the walls for a moment and went out.

Kara and Devon were left in the darkness. After a moment, Kara's eyes adjusted to the blackness around her. With the M-suit she could see better in the dark than when she was alive. She guessed this was how cats saw in the darkness.

"Let's go, *freak*." Devon sauntered towards the door leading to the basement.

"Wait!" cried Kara. "Shouldn't we use a moonstone for some light? It's pretty dark in here."

"No, moron. We don't want anyone to know we're here. Unless you're looking to die — then by all means ... light one up."

Kara made an obscene gesture behind his back. *I really do hate this guy.*

Grateful that her eyes were adjusting better to the darkness, she followed Devon through the doorway and down a flight of stairs. A wall of blackness hit her. The basement was nearly pitch black. She could only make out a few feet in front of her. The sound of their boots scraping the floors echoed around them. Kara couldn't tell where the basement walls ended and where they began. She could see Devon's back move up and down in a rhythmic motion.

A hiss sounded from somewhere behind her.

Kara whipped her head around. Something moved in the shadows. She blinked and it was gone. Only darkness stared back at her. Were her eyes playing tricks on her? At times, back when she was mortal, she would wake up from a nightmare to see a black shape hovering before her eyes. It would freak her out, but as soon as she blinked, the shape would disappear, and she would be left staring at her empty room. Maybe this was the same thing. She wondered if Devon had seen it, too. She turned back around. Devon had disappeared.

"Hey, Devon? Devon!"

No answer came. Her voice echoed through the darkness. *What the hell?*

Kara leaned against the wall. This must be part of Devon's plan. He would try and kill her here. This was his chance. He was probably hiding in the shadows ready to strike at any moment. She cursed herself for being so foolish. She thought about going back.

Something moved in the shadows.

Kara flattened herself against the wall. She reached inside her jacket and drew another soul blade. She wielded the two blades before her. She strained to see. She wasn't about to let herself be beaten down by Devon. She would get him first. Gently she pushed herself off the wall and took a step. She concentrated on the sounds around her — a drip of water from an old pipe, the screeching of metal against metal — but no Devon.

Red eyes flashed in the darkness.

A dark shape rose. Kara could just discern the shadow of a human form, small and childlike. It was bent like an insect. Abnormally long arms brushed the ground. Claws scraped the concrete floors. A low cackle sounded in the darkness. The foul smell of rotten flesh burned her nostrils — a demon.

The red eyes moved lower, and Kara could see the demon crouch down, about to leap. She leaned forward and steadied her arms. She was ready.

Hands grabbed Kara by the throat, and she flew into the air. She crashed against the wall behind her and slipped to the ground. The hands wrapped themselves around her throat. Her neck was on fire. She lifted her blades and hacked at the limbs around her neck. The demon let go.

She heard the sound of scraping to her right. Ignoring the pain in her neck, she flailed her arms in front of her, cutting through the darkness like a mad woman. Kara strained to see, but it was no use. There was only darkness. Another cackle of laughter caught her attention. Her anger rose. It was taunting her. The demon knew she couldn't see it.

Kara reached deep inside and called upon her elemental power. She desperately tried to tap into that energy she knew was hidden inside her soul. And once again, it let her down.

Frustrated, Kara cursed herself for not bringing a moonstone. Her only weapons were her two soul blades, and they weren't exactly helping her to see. Red eyes danced before her. The demon was enjoying itself.

Pain pierced at her back. She staggered forward. Her back was on fire. Kara cried out in excruciating pain. She turned and swung her blades at her invisible foe. But she only cut the air.

She steadied herself. Another pair of red eyes watched her from above. It hung from the ceiling like a fly. Now there were two of them. What were these demons? She felt the panic rise in her. How was she to fight back when she couldn't see? She was an easy prey for them.

A scraping sound came from down the hallway. Kara counted a dozen more pairs of red eyes coming her way. She didn't have time to think. There were too many. Too many, and it was too dark. They would be upon her in seconds. The sound of their gaping maws echoed in the dark. The hairs on her arms rose.

Kara whipped around and pushed her blade into a demon's eye. Wetness sprayed her face. The creature let out an ear-piercing wail. With her other blade, she slashed at where she imagined its head would be. She heard a soft thud, like a chunk of meat hitting the floor. The demon crumbled at her feet. She jumped over it and dashed down the hallway. She didn't stop to see if the others had chased her. The eerie scraping of claws against the concrete floor sounded behind her.

Kara ran blindly down the hallway. She stretched out her left hand and ran her finger tips against the wall. Suddenly the wall ended. Kara dashed into the opening to her left. Something caught her foot, and she crashed into some kind of glass wall. Shattered pierces of glass exploded all around her as she fell onto the floor. She staggered to her feet, shaken. She felt something in her head. She reached up and pulled a large shard of glass out of her forehead. Light poured from the gash. Kara was able to see a little. Chunks of glass poked out from her M-5 suit. She was covered in broken glass. She could hear the demons approaching. She didn't have time to remove the glass.

With the little light coming from her forehead, Kara bolted down another hallway. She could still hear the demons' claws scraping the floors behind her. The putrid smell of rot reached her nose again, and she sensed hot breath near the nape of her neck.

They were close.

Kara ran down more halls and through corridors. She passed many openings and rooms that were littered with junk. She couldn't see beyond that. She had just enough light to see five feet in front of her. The M-5 series were strong, and Kara was thankful she hadn't tired — just yet. But one thing was for sure — Kara knew she was lost.

She was deep into the bowels of the asylum. With the demons on her trail, her prospects didn't look very good. But she was determined to find her way out. She knew she was in the basement. She needed to find stairs to go up to the next level. At least on the first floor she could jump out of a window if she had to. She doubted whether she could find enough water to make the plunge back to Horizon. If she had some luck on her side, maybe she could find some washrooms. There had to be washrooms in this enormous building — maybe on the upper floors. Yes. Kara increased her speed and ran down the corridor — a dead end.

The hallway stopped abruptly. A large white wall stared back at her. She remembered passing an opening only moments before. There was no escape. She would have to fight her way out through a corridor of demons.

Kara whirled around and brandished her soul blades. She wouldn't go down without a fight.

At least thirty demons scurried towards her. There were too many. Some crawled from the ceiling and the walls. Glowing red eyes flashed with hunger. She would cut as many as she could and make a run for the doorway. The light coming from her forehead illuminated them clearly. They were definitely humanoid, with unusually large heads and slimy black skin that covered their skeletal bodies. They looked bent and broken, with abnormally long arms that dragged behind them as they crawled closer. Their foul smell burned into Kara's nose like acid.

They lunged.

Kara lifted her blades and struck down as many times as she could. Their claws ripped at her head, her limbs. They were trying to rip her apart. Kara slashed off the hands that tried to grab her face. Pain erupted in her side. She cried out. Three demons had their mouths attached to her sides. They were eating her m-flesh — they were eating her. She tried to call out to her power, but she was too frightened. There were just too many. Her panic rose as she hacked away at their black limbs. Her face was wet with their blood.

More demons came.

She felt the weight of a dozen or more bodies on top of her. Their hands covered her eyes. They pulled at her head. She felt her soul blades yanked from her hands. Panic engulfed her. She wasn't going to make it out.

Then they were gone.

Kara stumbled and fell. She looked around. The demons had vanished. She examined herself. Large gashes and bite marks covered her entire body. Light spilled from the many wounds. Her M-5 suit was stronger than the regular suits, but she felt that it had been damaged. The demons had done a number on it. She pushed herself up and staggered back towards where she had last seen an opening —

Hands grabbed her.

"Got her."

Kara thrashed around. Devon and Al held her tightly by her arms.

"What are you doing? Let me go." Kara struggled against their grip, but she couldn't pull free. She was lifted in the air and carried down the hall. She kicked and screamed as hard as she could. She smiled when she hit Al in the face with her boot. A soft yellow light poured from a room up ahead. They dragged Kara through a doorway and into the room, never letting her go.

The room was filled with old rusted medical equipment. Jars of blue and yellow liquid covered the entire back wall. A single metal bathtub stood at the far end of the room. Large metal restraints were welded into the concrete floor and against the wall behind the tub. Another pair of metal restraints dangled from the ceiling by a chain above the tub. Dark stains covered the floor at the foot of the bath. A chill passed through Kara. This is where they experimented on the patients.

Cassiel stood with his arms crossed over his chest. "Ah. There she is." He lifted his brows. "And injured, as I hoped she would be."

And then it hit her. This was supposed to happen. Like an idiot, she had been lured into another trap. "You wanted this to happen to me," Kara spit the words out of her mouth. "Didn't you?"

Cassiel smiled and pointed to the tub. "Put her in."

Devon and Al threw Kara into the bathtub. They pinned her down easily and fastened the restraints. Kara pulled at her restraints.

"Of course. I wanted you weak. Otherwise, we wouldn't be able to kill you."

Kara scrambled around and managed to sit up. "How ... how can you do this," she hissed. "You're an archangel! You're sworn to protect the mortals! Let go of me!" Kara kicked with her feet as hard as she could.

Cassiel shook his head. "Ah ... Kara ... Kara ... Kara. How little you know. The mortals are the problem, dear girl. Don't you see? For thousands of years we have been forced to save their miserable souls. And for what? What do we get from it? Nothing. Why should we waste our energy on lesser beings? Why should we care about their mundane lives?"

He walked over to the shelves and grabbed a large white plastic bottle. He read the label and shook the contents. "Do you know what this is?" He turned and sauntered towards the tub.

"Who cares?" Kara's anger flared. Cassiel's betrayal ran deep. "I trusted you. How could you! Get me out of this, Cassiel."

"I'm afraid not." He unscrewed the top. "You see my dear, I need to get you out of the way. You're the only one with enough power to do some real damage to our lord. And we can't have that now, can we?"

Kara pulled at her chains. "You're following the words of a madman. Can't you see? This is madness. The mortals are not the enemy. Asmodeus is!"

Cassiel held up the bottle for Kara to see. "This here is acid. Just a drop burns through metal." He smiled wickedly at Kara. "Your mortal suit will melt away within seconds. You'll be left without a shell — an easy kill. It'll be quick, I promise."

Kara watched Cassiel tip the bottle. "Stop!" she cried desperately. "The Legion will find out. You'll pay for this." She tried to stall for time.

The archangel laughed softly. "How can they? There won't be anything left of you to be discovered." Cassiel tipped the bottle.

A scraping sound came from beyond the threshold.

Suddenly, a large dog lunged at Cassiel's throat.

The archangel staggered sideways, and dropped the bottle. It splashed onto the floor, barely missing the tub. Cassiel fell to the ground as the great dog tore at his neck. Cassiel was lost in a layer of dark brown fur. But the archangel was strong. He tore the dog from his body and snapped its neck. He tossed the dead dog to the side. A smirk materialized on his face, pleased at his success.

Four more dogs appeared.

The giant dogs all leaped onto Cassiel. The canines tore at the archangel's flesh with incredible force. The weight of the great beasts forced him down. His eyes were wide with terror.

Fear rose in Kara's breast as she watched the dogs rip and tear away at the archangel. With a great pull, Cassiel lost an arm. Kara's jaw dropped.

Devon and Al jumped to his aid. They slashed their black blades at the dogs. But the dogs didn't stop. More dogs charged into the room. They didn't even glance at Kara. Their eyes were fixed on the others. Kara counted a dozen giant dogs. They leaped into the air and opened their massive jaws. The sound of tearing flesh froze her in her place. She had never witnessed such a terrifying scene. She loved dogs. She never imagined how scary they could be when they were angry.

Cassiel managed to push off his attackers. He fled through the door without looking back. He abandoned his teammates.

The bodies of Devon and Al disappeared as the dogs ate them. Then they turned their eyes to Kara, and she felt a shiver roll up her back. Were they coming to eat her now?

A white and tan dog trotted in. He was short and bulky, with a large square head. His tongue hung on the side of his jaw. He walked up to the tub and sniffed.

"You look like hell. If you really needed a bath, I could have helped you with that," said the dog.

Kara collapsed in relief. "Thor! I'm so glad to see you."

The bulldog waddled along the floor and went to inspect the bottle. "Just in time I see. This is acid. You were about to become angel stew."

"How did you find me?"

Thor sat on his hind legs and began to scratch his ear. "Jenny sent me a message. She said you were on a rotten mission with some traitors. I followed your stench."

"Thanks."

"You're welcome. You're lucky you smell so bad, otherwise we might have missed you."

Kara didn't respond. She thought she smelled great. She glanced over at the great dogs. Some lay comfortably on the floor while others sat staring at her. They seemed to be listening in.

"Are they Scouts, like you?"

Thor jumped up and stretched proudly. "Yes. My comrades, the king shepherds."

Kara examined the dogs. They were all very large with long fluffy brown and black fur. The markings on their faces were distinctly those of a shepherd. "Thank you for saving my life."

"You're welcome," chorused the dogs. They seemed to smile at her. The largest of the group trotted over and dropped a key in her lap.

"Found this on one of the traitors. I almost swallowed it," said the large dog.

Kara thanked him and began to unlock her restraints.

Thor lifted his head and smelled the air. "Demons. We should get going."

Kara jumped out of the tub. She watched the shepherds file out together. She rubbed her wrists. "You don't have to ask me twice. This place gives me the creeps. Let's go."

CHAPTER 9
CASTELLO DI ZENA

News of Cassiel's treachery had spread throughout the Legion. As soon as Kara had made her way back to Horizon and reported what had happened, the Legion was in an uproar. It was bad enough that Zadkiel had been found to be a traitor, but now that Cassiel had been revealed as a traitor and murderer as well, the Legion's spirit was broken.

Kara sat at the round table in CDD. She drummed her fingers and watched the gloomy faces of her comrades. If Jenny could cry, Kara was sure she'd be in tears. Jenny had admired the archangel. She had looked up to him, and bragged about him constantly. Kara could see his betrayal had affected her deeply. Perhaps Jenny had cared more about him than she let on.

Peter wasn't in a much better shape. He sat with his back to the group. He refused to speak to anyone and mumbled continually to himself. His glasses rested on the table. With his head down, he stared at his feet, lost in his thoughts. Kara felt an immense sadness for him. She wanted to go over and wrap her arms around him. But something inside told her to leave him be. Jenny and Peter had known Cassiel longer than she had. They needed time to mourn without the new girl interfering.

But the field agents weren't the only ones affected. The entire division moped around. It was like being at a funeral. The depression threatened to spread like a virus. Missions weren't being assigned, and Kara felt the division had lost its spark. CDD was leaderless.

A sudden commotion got Kara's attention. She stood up, excited. Gabriel strode towards her. Cassiel had been large, but Kara had forgotten how much more massive Gabriel was than the other archangels. His tight black shirt wrapped around his chest and revealed his powerful body. His muscles rippled as he walked. With his black cargo pants and large black boots, he was dressed as a field agent just like them.

Kara could see a head of blonde hair behind Gabriel's shoulder. She leaned to the left to get a better view of who was following the archangel. A flutter passed through her. She pressed her lips together tightly, afraid to let a giant smile escape. David sauntered towards them, with a cheeky smile on his face. Kara could see that he was happy, just by the way he walked, with his head held high. He had wanted to join the CDD for years, and Kara had always felt a little uncomfortable that she had been allowed in, and not David. Gabriel had said that David's reputation for being difficult and disobedient had affected his chances. But now, here he was, proud as a peacock.

No one moved as the tread of Gabriel and David's boots echoed through the chamber. Gabriel turned and eyed the room silently. He met Kara's eyes and nodded. Kara did the same. She watched as David settled beside him. He noticed her looking, and gave her a wink. Kara bit her lip, so as not to laugh, but a soft snort escaped her anyway. Embarrassed, she looked around, but no one seemed to be paying any attention to her. The divisions' attention was on Gabriel.

The archangel surveyed the room once more before he spoke. "Guardians. The Legion can't afford to have you looking like sad little puppies. Yes, Cassiel is gone. Yes, it was a shock to us all ... but that doesn't mean this division is finished. CDD is still operational. The threat is still out there. Mortals are dying, guardians! Snap out of it right now!" Gabriel's voice boomed throughout the chamber like thunder. Kara's skin prickled.

"Your orders are to find the demon lord's command center. We know he's there—his demons need direct contact with him. We need to locate that post. I want you to report back right away, once you have a positive ID on the location. Don't let them see you. We need the element of surprise on our side, when we are ready to strike."

Kara wondered how they were to strike Asmodeus. It was one thing to find his location, but how were they planning to defeat him? He had two fallen archangels on his team and a huge multitude of demons. He had already proved to be more powerful than expected. The Legion must have some idea as to how they were going to put an end to him.

Gabriel's face was tight and determined. "You are the best there is, so prove it. Now is not the time to feel sorry for yourselves. You are warriors! We are at war and the Legion needs you."

Kara looked around. Gabriel's little pep talk seemed to have done the trick. Kara saw new life spark in Jenny's and Peter's eyes, and she felt the excitement flow into her own body too.

"Back to your duties, everyone," announced Gabriel. "I want possible locations in five minutes. Field agents, get ready to jump soon."

Immediately, the room was alive with the sound of angels running to the desks and calling out names of cities to scan. Holographic screens sprouted back to life with colorful maps of cities around the globe. Kara smiled. It was nice to see CDD operational again.

"What's up, cutie?" Kara turned to meet a smiling David. "Do you want to see my ... badge?" David flipped open his CDD identification, as though he were a detective flashing his badge. His eyes gleamed with satisfaction. He had never looked so pleased.

Kara laughed softly. "I see you've finally made it to the big leagues. I thought you were a lost cause. What made the Legion change its mind?"

"Ultimately, it was the High Council's decision, but Gabriel persuaded them—told them they needed an angel with spectacular fighting skills—not to mention my good looks."

Kara's eyes lowered, and she focused on David's full lips. She felt a sudden pull towards them. Kara met David's stare. A flutter of excitement rose in her breast. Kara found that she couldn't look away from those brilliant blue eyes. Unaware of the curious eyes around them, she felt herself leaning in —

"Ahem."

Kara pulled back and turned. Gabriel examined her with raised eyebrows. "Glad to see you in one piece, Kara."

"Uh … hi, Gabriel," she managed to croak. She looked at David. "I was just congratulating David on his promotion to CDD. I know how much it means to him." She could see a huge smile emerge on David's face.

"Yes, I'm sure. We are all very pleased with his advancement. Although not as delighted as David himself." Gabriel's black eyes pierced Kara's, and she thought she could see a shadow of a smile appear on his lips.

"Sir!" A tall guardian with tanned skin and short curly hair ran up to the archangel. "We found two possible locations of the demon lord, sir." He handed some papers to Gabriel who studied each of them closely.

After a moment, the archangel looked up and addressed the field agents. "Listen up. I want two teams ready to go to these locations — an abandoned church in Spain and an old castle in Italy. Peter and Jenny —" Gabriel flung out his arm, a piece of paper dangled from his fingers. "You're the first team. On your feet!"

Peter jumped from his chair and took the paper. He studied it for a moment and then gave it to Jenny to read. Kara watched her eyes light up after she read it.

"And the second team," Kara heard Gabriel say. "Kara … and David."

Kara heard whispers amongst the division. She couldn't quite catch what they were saying, but she knew it had something to do with her being teamed up with David.

"You are to scout the areas first, and then report back. No funny business … I don't want any fooling around. I want both teams back safely. Got that? You've got an hour." Gabriel's eyes focused on David.

David grabbed the last piece of paper from Gabriel's hand. Kara leaned over and read:

Castello di Zena,
Italy

Italy sounded interesting to her. An old decrepit castle would be perfect. Kara imagined Asmodeus sitting on his throne, his demons bowing down before him, with mortal souls as offerings. It was the perfect location. Fit for a demon king.

"You ready?" David cocked his head and searched her face. "I'm dying to try the tanks."

Kara let the overly enthusiastic David drag her down to the platform where the vega tanks awaited them. She couldn't help but laugh as he hauled her away. Peter and Jenny were already positioned behind the wall of green waters.

"Good luck! And be careful." Kara waved at them both. Peter waved back and Jenny gave her two thumbs up. They disappeared in a flash of white light.

David jumped up onto the platform. "Let's go. I'm so ready for this." He rubbed his hands together as though he was about to start a fire with his bare hands. "Can't wait to try one of these babies."

Kara laughed again and stepped up onto the dais.

Gabriel's dark eyes glared at David. "David, stop acting like a jackass. You think you could try to act like a guardian for once, and not an idiot," he called, "I had to do a lot of convincing to let you in CDD. Don't make me regret my decision. Don't make me out to be a fool, David McGowan."

"I won't, big daddy. Promise." David beamed at him. He skipped into the air like a little girl with a jump rope. Kara saw Gabriel's mood darken.

"David, don't be a moron," Kara whispered. "Try to be serious, just this once. Can you do that?"

David stepped up to a vega tank. "Don't worry, Gabe. We'll be back in one piece. I can promise you that. We'll be back before you've had the chance to miss us — cause I know you will."

"You better," grunted Gabriel. "Good luck to you. Be safe."

"You ready?" David turned his head to Kara and arched his brows.

Kara straightened her back and stepped to David's left behind a tank.

She nodded. "Ready."

Together, they walked into the green waters and vanished.

Moments later, Kara strolled amidst tall grasses that swayed back and forth in a soft breeze. David came running up before her, did a summersault, and dashed back into the grass. Kara shook her head and sighed. He was blatantly mad. David ran and laughed like a crazy person, pushing the M-5 suit's strength and enjoying every bit of it.

It was midday, and the sun's rays pierced through openings in the tall evergreens. Buds of light green covered the trees; a hint of spring lingered in the air. Green hills rolled out for miles in every direction and out of sight. Kara heard the sound of rolling water. A small creek wound through the hills and disappeared into the thick forest. Tall trees with yellow leaves flickered in the sun like gold.

But then Kara noticed that the forest was unnaturally silent, as though no animals lived there. Kara couldn't hear any birds or squirrels busying themselves with the coming of spring. It wasn't normal—something was amiss.

Hiding in a valley of tangled forest, was the abandoned Italian castle, Castello di Zena. It was a mystery falling to pieces, resplendent in the tall grass. Overgrown vines scaled the sides of the castle walls and up the keep, as though draping it with leaves to keep it warm. Large boulders lay crumbled at the base of the castle. A whole east wall had fallen over with time and was now the home to weeds and shrubs.

Kara felt pressure on her arm. She turned around. David had his finger to his lips and pulled her down with him behind a large bush. He pointed to the castle. Kara scanned the grounds. Dark shadows moved amongst the tall grasses. Demons. There were demons everywhere. Four giant demons that resembled bears, but with yellow horns protruding from their heads, guarded the main entrance. Kara counted a dozen more walking the grounds. But that wasn't the worse part. Hundreds of lesser demons crawled and snaked around the castle, their bodies swollen and infected; leaving dark stains on the grounds. Kara felt suddenly sick. She noticed that the demons never ventured too far away, always keeping to the grounds. The castle was heavily protected. Kara knew they were protecting something precious inside the castle.

She felt the hairs on her arms rise. Asmodeus was in there, she was sure of it. Kara pictured the demon lord on a golden throne with a jeweled crown, slicing the throats of every angel that didn't bow down and kiss his feet. Kara was anxious to share a little father-daughter time. She had a lot on her mind.

"I bet he's in there," whispered David, knocking Kara out of her trance. "It wouldn't be so heavily guarded if he wasn't."

"Should we report back?"

David shook his head. "No. We need to be one hundred percent sure he's in there. For all we know, this could be a decoy. We have to try to get in somehow."

Kara inspected the main entrance again. Four massive demons were not impossible to fight, but the hundreds of lesser demons joining in would be. If things started to get complicated with the larger demons, she knew the others would be upon them in a blink of an eye. Not a great plan — they would have to sneak in somehow. There had to be another way in. Everyone knew castles had secret entryways and miles of underground tunnels. They would just have to find one.

"Let's go around and see if there's another way in that's less guarded."

"Good idea."

David led the way, and the two of them slid down a long slope and landed in two feet of wet marsh. After Kara voiced her disgust they stealthily made their way around the east side of the castle. Still fighting their way through the marshes, they passed the fallen east wall, and David motioned for Kara to stop. He threw out his arm. Kara saw that he pointed to a small opening behind a stone wall. It must have been a doorway once, Kara thought. The demons didn't seem interested in the area; they were all still watching the front of the castle.

Kara looked at David and nodded.

David drew a soul blade. It sparkled in the sun and blinded Kara for a moment. He clenched his jaw. Kara could tell by the deep frowns on his forehead that he was thinking hard. A real warrior, she thought as she watched him step out of the marshes. She was glad they were a team again. Kara brandished her blade and followed closely behind him.

With hunched backs, they made their way across the grounds as quietly as they could. Kara threw nervous glances behind her as they hurried across the grasses.

No demons came.

They were almost there. Kara could make out the white-washed walls of bird droppings as they moved closer to the castle. A rotted door lay but a few feet from the opening. The hinges were still attached, a reminder of where the door once had been. David jumped over large rocks and debris. Kara followed closely behind.

A sudden earsplitting wail erupted all around them.

Kara froze in her tracks. The howl had come from behind her. David spun around. Kara saw fear flash in his eyes momentarily. She tightened her hold on her dagger and turned around. A horde of grotesque monsters with extra heads and gaping maws with razor sharp fangs stared back at her. Beasts of the Netherworld gathered around them. Some had humanoid shapes while others were animal-like. They drummed the wet earth with their twisted limbs. Smaller demons with black oily skin crept out of the forest. Kara's skin crawled. She recognized the demons she had faced in the asylum. Hunger flashed in their red eyes. Hundreds of bent shapes gathered. It was an army of demons.

Kara recoiled at the stench of rotten flesh. Her eyes burned.

Another wail cut through the air, louder than all the other sounds. Kara heard an eerie answer to the call. The ground rumbled. More demons came. The demons were calling in backup.

David pulled out a firestone from his jacket. "Kara—stay close!"

He threw the red globe into the mass of oncoming demons. There was a thundering boom, and red light detonated. Chunks of demon flesh flew into the air and sprayed the grounds in black liquid. Other demons roared angrily. A large demon with a bull's body and lizard head sprang in attack. Its yellow eyes were fixed on Kara. Droplets of black slime slipped off its body as it charged.

Kara readied herself. The beast attacked. She smelled its sour breath as it neared. In the next moment, she side-stepped, twisted her body, lifted her arm and slashed her blade. The beast's body crumbled to the ground. Its head rolled off.

"Not bad." David laughed nervously. "You think you could do that again ... a few hundred times? Watch out!"

Kara felt a stabbing pain on her leg. She cried out. A small demon had latched itself onto her leg, and was chomping away at her M-suit's skin. She stabbed it in the head and threw it off easily. She thought about making a run for the opening, but more demons blocked their way. Kara felt panic rise in her. They were surrounded.

"Any genius plans, David? Now would be the time." She reached inside her jacket pocket, from which she pulled a firestone. "I've got only one of these."

David's face was grim. "Maybe this wasn't such a good idea. We need backup. You think we could make a run for it to the hills?"

"Let's do it."

Kara threw her firestone into the wall of demons. There was an explosion, and suddenly a clear path. Kara knew it would last only a few seconds. She pushed her M-5 suit as hard as it would go and dashed towards the hills, slashing at the demons that stood in her way. She was surprised at her own strength. Nothing seemed to stop her. She only looked back once she was out of the demons' reach.

"David, I think we're—"

David was not there. Panic overwhelmed her.

"David!"

Kara ran back down the hill. Desperately, she searched for David. But he was nowhere to be found. Anger replaced her fear. She flew over tree stumps and rocks as she ran towards the demons at the bottom of the hill. They were piled on top of one another, slashing at something beneath them. There was a struggle, then a scream. She recognized the scream.

David was underneath them.

CHAPTER 10
THE HIDDEN TRUTHS

Horrified, Kara screamed in rage. Her vision blurred in her madness. She felt the elemental power within her waken. She called to it as she ran. It answered. She thought only of saving David. Nothing else mattered. Not Asmodeus. Not the Legion. Just David.

Kara dashed down the rest of the hill. She could see David's arms flailing beneath the throng of demons who held him down. They tore at his flesh. Kara heard him scream again. She flinched at his pain. They were hurting him.

She was almost there.

Her vision changed, and everything was covered with hues of gold. Kara rejoiced in her power. She would destroy every last one of them. She tossed her soul blade. She didn't need it anymore. With a final jump, Kara landed in front of the mass of creatures. Her wrath burned at her core. She only saw death. Her fury escaped with a thunderous roar.

"No!"

Golden light flickered and danced in her palms like electricity. The demons stopped and looked up.

"Get away from him!" Kara threw out her hands, ready to launch her attack—

Then she recoiled.

The demons scattered away from David, suddenly, as though they were frightened. They fixed their eyes on Kara; they waited.

"What the hell?" David sat up and rubbed his head.

Kara noticed a few bite marks, but other than that he appeared to be fine.

"What did you do? How did you make them listen to you?"

Kara was dumbfounded. She hadn't even released her power. She had only told them to get away, and they had listened to her. Kara strained to keep her emotions intact, her elemental power ready and waiting within her, just in case she needed it. But the demons had done what she asked. They had backed away from David, and were standing there—waiting. It was as though she was their master somehow. She decided to test out her theory a little further.

"Demons, I want you all to sit down—and be still—until I tell you to move." Kara watched anxiously as the entire mass of demons sat down. It worked again. They obeyed her.

"Well, I'm glad I had an M-5 series on." David inspected his body with a silly grin. "Otherwise, I think I would have been reduced to angel jam."

He pushed himself up and walked over to the closest demon. "Let's test this further, shall we?" It was a pitiful creature with no eyes and a large gaping mouth full of yellow teeth. Black liquid oozed from the many sores around its body. David stabbed it with his blade. The creature howled, twitched, and then fell over, dead.

"Interesting. The little bugger didn't even fight back. How did you do this, Kara? It's as if they're listening to you — you've somehow become their boss. I mean, why now and not before … what's different?"

Kara shrugged. David had a point. "I don't know. I told them to stop … and they did. It just happened." And then it hit her. She knew. With the elemental energy still flowing freely inside her, she felt another presence inside, like a bond. She felt a connection to these creatures somehow, and she knew without a doubt that the demons felt the same connection to her. They recognized her elemental power. She was the one who had released them into the mortal world. She was their master.

"I think I know why." Kara looked at David.

She turned away, afraid of what he might think when she told him. "They're connected to me somehow … because of my elemental power. It was my power that allowed them to cross over into the mortal world. And I think they recognized it when it surfaced. I think … I know they will do as I say."

David pursed his lips. "Very interesting. Might come in handy. So they'll just sit there and wait?"

"I think so." Kara surveyed the demons. A gentle breeze brought with it the stink of rotten flesh and something more revolting that Kara didn't want to think about. Hundreds of pairs of red eyes watched her silently. Intelligence reflected back in some of them, whereas others had only a bleak expression. Some were just bodies without consciousness, twisted and misshapen.

They waited patiently for her instructions. She thought of the only thing that made sense.

"Demons. I command you to leave the mortal world. I want you to go back to the Netherworld and stay there. You must never return here, and you must never hurt a human being again. Now go."

David came to stand by Kara. They both watched in wonder as the creatures got up swiftly and disappeared into the forest one by one. In less than three minutes, the grounds were empty.

Flocks of multicolored birds chirped happily and squirrels chattered as they chased one another up a pine tree. The air smelled of pine needles and spring blossoms. There were no more traces of demons anywhere.

"Nice job." David's eyes glistened. "Think you could do that to all the demons? Maybe even higher demons?"

Kara brushed the hair from her eyes. "I don't think I can control higher demons. I think this only worked because these are the *same* demons Asmodeus released by using the mirror … and me. I doubt it'll work on new breeds or higher demons."

"Well, that's too bad. But I'm glad it worked for this stinking lot." David shrugged and searched inside his jacket. He pulled out a blade. "I wonder what Gabriel's gonna say about all this."

Kara frowned. It still felt a little strange that she had been able to control those demons. She didn't want to be associated with Asmodeus. If the Legion found out, would they think she was playing for the other team? Was this what Zadkiel had meant about her being more demon than angel? She wasn't sure how she felt about all this. She was glad it had worked, but it left her wondering if there was something more to being part elemental than she knew, if she was ready to accept it.

"David, do you think you can keep this between us? Until I figure out what to do about it. I don't know what Gabriel or the Legion would think about my new *ability*. Can we keep this just between the two of us for now, please?"

David looked at Kara kindly. "Of course, Kara. I won't say anything if you don't want me to. They don't need to know about this. I'll leave this part out of my report to the big man, don't worry," he laughed softly. "Probably wouldn't even believe me anyway."

Relieved, Kara stared at the dark opening on the east side wall of the castle. "Do you still want to check it out?" Kara glanced at her watch. "We still have a half hour before we have to report back."

"Yeah ... I think we should." David dusted off his jacket. "We can't leave without knowing if he's in there or not. I don't want to disappoint the big man on my first mission as a CDD field agent. I can't do any more begging ... it's beginning to affect my reputation."

Kara ignored him. She looked down at her hands and wondered if this new ability was part of Asmodeus's plan. Was he going to use her to control the demons on Earth? What if he, too, could feel what she just did to his demons? If he did, that meant he might be waiting for them inside the castle. The elemental power had already left her, and she didn't have any other weapons. She brushed the tall grass with her boots and searched for her soul blade.

David handed her his blade. "Here — take this one. We don't have time to search for yours. I have another one." Kara took the blade and clasped it in her hand.

"Thanks."

"Let's go inside and look for lord dumbass."

Kara followed David along a small stone walkway overgrown by weeds and grass. It led to the opening in the wall. Large jagged rocks projected from the top like fangs, a warning to those who dared to enter. Kara shivered involuntarily. Hiding her fears from David, she followed him in.

They stood in a dark lobby with narrow walls. Soft light flickered from the lanterns on the walls. Someone or something had been in there for sure; they had taken the time to fire up the lanterns. Dirt covered the floor like a grey carpet. The air was hot and stuffy. Kara suddenly felt claustrophobic. She didn't want to stay there for much longer. Thankfully, David crept forward and the air cleared up a bit.

They walked silently for ten minutes, both with their weapons out and ready. The light from the torches flickered on their soul blades. They didn't meet any other demons. The tunnel was as silent as a grave. Every so often they would pass collapsed walls. And Kara wondered what supported the upper levels. The light weakened up ahead. David slowed down and pressed his body against the wall. Kara followed his example. Together, they moved slowly towards the waning light, careful not to make any sudden loud crunching noises with their boots.

They entered a large round chamber. Yellow light spilled in from the roofless top. A large pile of flat stones lay crushed on the floor. The roof, Kara guessed. Weeds sprouted from cracked floor stones in a tile pattern of moss green. Trees had found spaces to grow and flourish in the room. Four stone columns rose from the ground and reached the open sky. Birds' nests rested on the tops like crowns made of straw. Bird droppings painted the floors and columns in a sticky whitewash.

A raised marble platform stood in the center of the room. A great wooden chair with carved legs in the shape of lion's paws, rested upon the dais.

A man sat in the chair.

Slumped casually against the chair, he gazed at them with dark, unblinking eyes. He wore a light grey suit and light pink tie. His hair was dark brown and cut short. He wasn't moving.

"Stay behind me." David walked towards the man cautiously. He balanced his soul blade between his fingers. With each new step he looked around the room nervously, as if expecting to be ambushed any second.

Kara felt something was wrong. Something was definitely wrong with the man, but she couldn't figure out what. The closer she got, the stronger she felt that something was amiss. She looked over her shoulder nervously. What if this was a trap? Still the man didn't move or blink.

Flies buzzed around her face, and she waved them away impatiently. She bumped into David's back. His face was drawn into a frown. Kara realized he was staring at the man. She stepped aside and gasped.

A mortal man sat in the chair. His flesh was dark grey and covered in sores. Decaying flesh peeled away from his face and hands, leaving exposed wet wounds. Large gashes oozed green pus. Buzzing sounds echoed around them. He was covered in flies. The smell of rotten flesh burned Kara's nostrils. His eyes had been removed, Kara noticed. But it was the expression on his face that terrified her. It was frozen in an expression of pure terror. Kara knew he had suffered. Sadness welled inside her. He didn't deserve this. No mortal deserved to die and be exposed like this. A single yellow post-it was stuck to his forehead.

Kara edged closer and read;

Your love for the monkeys has blinded you from the truth

"What does that mean?" David ripped off the post-it, crumpled it and threw it on the ground. "Is this some sick joke? You think this is funny—you demon lunatic!" His voice carried throughout the chamber.

Kara picked up the creased note and evened it out against her thigh. She studied it for a moment. "It doesn't make sense. Why go through all this trouble? Why was this place guarded if he was never here?"

David kicked the chair. "Because he's a sick bastard! This is a game to him! He's probably hiding somewhere having a good laugh."

But Kara wasn't convinced. None of this made any sense.

"But why hide? He's supposed to be strong, right? He believes he's more powerful and cleverer than any of us. He's not afraid of you or me, or the Legion. It—it just doesn't make any sense." She thought for a moment, and then she read the note again out loud, desperately trying to decipher the meaning.

"I'm telling you, he's mocking us! He's not here. It's just me, you, and this poor bastard." David smoothed the top of his hair down with his hands. Kara thought he was going a little mad.

Kara squinted down at the note. It was written in the form of a riddle. She was never good at cracking riddles. Their hidden meanings always gave her a headache. "Would a king hide away from a weaker opponent? No. Asmodeus is smart ... really smart. He's testing us with this, I'm sure of it. This note is a clue. It means something ... I ... I just can't figure it out."

"It means we're fools."

Kara ignored David as she focused on the note. She kept repeating the words over and over again inside her head until she chanted them. The truth. What was the truth? *Your love for the monkeys has blinded you from the truth.* And then it hit her.

Kara's face paled. "David. I know what it means."

David whipped his head around and stared at her with wide eyes. "So … tell me? What's the dumbass trying to tell us?"

Kara crumbled the note in her hand. She stared at the floor for a moment, as though preparing herself for what she was about to say. "It means … he was never after the mortal world. The attack on the mortal world was just a diversion."

Kara watched the realization flicker across David's face. She knew he thought she was right. "Think about it. He hates mortals. Why would he want to control a world filled with so-called monkeys? That's something he never wanted. He's been planning this all along." Kara met David's eyes.

"He's going after Horizon."

CHAPTER II
THE 8TH PLANE

David's eyes were cold and determined. "We have to warn them." He secured his blade inside his jacket. "We have to move fast, Kara. I saw a creek not too far away from the castle. Let's move."

Kara only nodded, still numb with the truth of what she had discovered. It was the truth. As soon as the words had escaped her lips, she knew it was true. She shivered. Her dear father was going after Horizon.

They ran back through the tunnels and out through the east side of the castle, faster than Kara would have imagined possible. The M-5 suits proved themselves yet again. The sky was a dark brown, and Kara instantly knew without looking at her watch that they had taken up their full hour. Gabriel had warned them to be back within an hour. Jenny and Peter were probably already back from their mission by now. Most probably they'd announced that their location was a decoy — and had been left wondering if Kara's and David's was the real deal. No one would have suspected that Horizon was the real target. Asmodeus had played his cards right. The question was: when did he plan on striking?

They galloped across the main grounds, and Kara soon heard the soft rush of the creek. Most of the Legion's guardians were out in the mortal world, saving lives. They had left Horizon unprotected. It would be an easy target. The father she hated had come up with a brilliant plan. It would be a massacre. The Legion would have to call in all the troops and ready themselves for an attack. She had to warn them. Time was running out.

Kara's mind raced faster than her legs. Gabriel would know what to do. They had to reach him first.

"There's the creek!" Kara heard David call up ahead.

The stream rushed down purposely, as if commanding them to make haste.

David grabbed Kara's hand and squeezed. "Ready?"

Kara squeezed back gently. "Ready."

Together they leaped into the air and landed with a loud splash in the icy spring waters.

Kara opened her eyes moments later.

A grey haze masked her vision. She blinked several times. She shivered and looked around. Fog lingered waist high above the ground. A thinner mist stirred slowly from above like moving clouds. It was everywhere. There was no sky, and no sun. The fog appeared to go on forever.

She looked down. Fog coiled around her legs like snakes. Through the vapors, her feet pressed down against grey concrete floors. She remembered having a dream like this once, where she stood alone and lost in a vast field of rolling fog. A strange metallic smell lingered in the air.

Something felt wrong to Kara. She was definitely not in an elevator, so where the heck was she? She had always found herself in one of the elevators with a snotty primate when she had jumped back from a mission. But there was no primate to greet her this time, just a field of fog. How did she get here?

She remembered David's handsome face. She remembered jumping into the creek with him moments ago. She couldn't see David anywhere.

"David! David, where are you?"

No reply.

Panicked, Kara ran blindly into the wall of fog calling out David's name but just an eerie echo answered her. *Strange*, she thought. She stopped running and flailed her arms in the fog, searching for David or anything solid. She cursed the mist.

A dull thud came from far in the distance. Kara strained her eyes to see through the mist. It was no use. It was like trying to see with a blanket over your face. Kara's chest tightened. Where was she? And what had happened to David?

She heard a tapping sound. It sounded like footsteps. They were coming towards her. She couldn't see. Who or what was coming towards her? The footsteps became louder. She remembered that she still carried one of David's soul blades, and she pulled it out. She waved the blade easily in her hand. No matter what was coming, she was going to put up a fight.

The wall of mist separated.

"Kara! Thank god." David's worried expression faded into one of intense relief. He rushed up to Kara and wrapped his arms around her. He squeezed her tenderly.

While she enjoyed being held by David, she pushed him back gently. "David, what happened? What is this place?"

David shook his head. "I have no freaking idea," he said warily. "Never been here before."

"Why didn't we make the leap to the elevators?" Kara looked around again, hoping to see the disapproving glare of one of the primates. But there was only fog, spread out as far as the eye could see.

"Something must have happened to disrupt our transition." David's face was tense. "I don't know where we are, but I know we're not in Horizon." David turned to Kara. "Is this the Netherworld?"

"No." Kara shrugged as she remembered the demon realm. Evil lurked in the shadows there, and voices had called out to her. She'd had an eerie feeling of malevolence following her in the Netherworld. She shook off the memory. "Trust me, the demon realm is foul—really foul. This … this feels … empty."

"Well, it's not exactly helping our cause." David paced, his face pulled tight. "If there's a way in—there's got to be a way out. We just have to find it."

Kara nodded. "You're right. We landed here somehow. There has to be a way out of this miserable fog." She whirled around on the spot. "Where do we start? Everywhere looks the same."

David glanced ahead. "Let's go this way." He pointed straight ahead. "Looks like the fog is clearing up. It might lead us somewhere."

Kara followed David closely, for fear of losing him in the thick mist.

A dark figure materialized before them.

Kara tensed and brandished her weapon. She watched David doing the same in the corner of her eye. They stood together, side-by-side, and waited.

The fog lifted, and the silhouette of a tall man glided towards them. He wore a long black robe that rippled behind him as he neared. A rope belt was tied around his waist, from which dangled a set of keys. She could hear the slight clang of them as he neared, but no footsteps. It was as though he floated. A hood kept his face in shadow, and when he got closer, Kara saw that he had no face. Kara shivered involuntarily — it looked demonic to her.

David stepped forward and waved his blade, a smile on his lips. "I wouldn't come any closer — monk — unless you're looking to meet your maker."

The being stood still, as though it was studying them. After a moment it spoke. "I am the Keeper," said the creature, and

Kara wondered how it could form a voice without a mouth to articulate words. The voice was hoarse and high pitched. Kara thought perhaps the Keeper was female. A very ugly female, she thought.

David cocked his head, but didn't lower his blade. "Keeper? Never heard of you. What kind of demon are you, Keeper? Keeper of souls? Keeper of little children?"

The Keeper shook its head. "I am not a demon, but a supernatural entity, like you."

"You're nothing like us." David glared at the creature. "Where are we, Keeper? And don't try any of your demon tricks."

The Keeper raised its arms before them. White skeletal hands appeared beneath rolls of sleeves. Thin translucent skin was stretched over the bones. "You are in the eighth plane. And I am its Keeper."

Kara leaned closer and grabbed a fist full of David's jacket. She whispered in his ear. "What's the eighth plane?" David shook his head and shrugged. Fear nipped the back of Kara's mind. But there was no time or place for fear. Her priority was to get the crucial information to the Legion, before Asmodeus attacked.

Uncertainty spread over David's face. "We've never heard of the eighth plane. Tell me, Keeper. How did we get here?"

The Keeper tilted its head to the side. "Just like all the other spirits before you … your supernatural bodies passed through the veil … and entered the eighth plane."

Kara didn't like that answer, and she was in no mood for more riddles. She thought she might have better luck with this creature than David did.

"Okay, so tell me. What *is* the eighth plane, Keeper?" asked Kara.

The Keeper folded its skeletal hands calmly before it. "The eighth plane is a realm for spirits that have lost their way. It is a place of refuge, a gathering. It is nowhere and everywhere at once."

It was Kara's time to step forward. She shook her head. "Wait a minute. So you're saying our spirits got lost? We got lost on the way back to Horizon?"

"Yes." The Keeper bowed its head lightly, and Kara thought it looked sad for a moment. "Unfortunately, your spirits couldn't reach Horizon. And so they have passed through the veil to the eighth plane."

"But how is that even possible?" David asked, and Kara could hear the frustration in his voice. She felt her own irritation rise. "Spirits can't get lost. There's no such thing as the eighth plane. You're lying. You're trying to trick us, demon! Tell us where we really are … are we in some demon realm?"

The Keeper stood quietly for a moment before answering. Kara noticed its fingers twitch, and she wondered if it was getting nervous. Only liars get nervous.

"I am not trying to trick you," continued the Keeper. "I am no demon trickster ... but the Keeper of the eighth plane. I'm afraid the doorways to Horizon have been closed."

Kara flinched. This couldn't be happening—not when the Legion's survival depended on them. She took a step forward toward the Keeper. She pointed to the creature with a trembling finger. "What do you mean by *closed*? How can they be closed? That's impossible!"

"There is an imbalance in the planes." The Keeper looked up into the endless fog, and Kara wondered where his eyes would be on that milky face.

"Something is happening in our spirit world at this very moment. This anomaly somehow has caused a fracture in the planes. That is why your bodies have come here ... to the eighth plane."

Panic ate through Kara, like acid eating through metal. "What anomaly? What fractured the planes?" Her father's image echoed in her mind. She tightened her grip on her blade.

"Only something of great power could tear a hole in the veil," answered the Keeper. "We are ... unsure of its origin ... we do not know where the source of this power comes from, but we are certain of the damage it has caused to our world."

Kara exchanged a look with David. She could tell by the look he gave her that they both agreed as to where this source came from, and who the source was. They had already wasted too much time speaking to the faceless Keeper. They needed to get out, and fast.

"There'll be more damage soon if you don't send us back quickly," pressed Kara. "We need to leave, and we need to leave right now. We have to warn them!"

The Keeper shook its head sadly. "I am sorry, but I cannot."

Kara's temper rose, and before David could interject, she cut him off. "You must! You don't understand. There is going to be a huge war. Angels are going to be killed. You have to send us back — now!"

"I'm sorry," repeated the Keeper, its voice gentle. "Once your spirit has entered the eighth plane, it can never go back. It will remain here … forever."

CHAPTER 12
⊕N STAGE

"This can't be happening!" Kara hit her head in frustration and stomped her feet. "There's got to be a way, there has to be! We can't stay here—we need to get back to Horizon, this instant!"

"I am truly, sorry." The Keeper lowered its head. It seemed to reflect for a moment. "You will find the eighth plane quite agreeable. This is merely a small portion of the plane. It can be … quite beautiful, in its own way."

Kara grabbed David's arm and turned him around. "David. We can't stay here! We have to warn the Legion." She fought to control her trembling, and squeezed his arm harder than she wanted.

David raked his fingers in his hair and yelled out in frustration. "Keeper. Tells us how to get out! There's a way in, so there must be a way out."

The Keeper just shook its head and didn't answer. Its face was expressionless and Kara wondered if it were laughing at them right now, hidden behind its white mask of a face. Perhaps this was a trickster demon who played with their emotions and deliberately kept their escape a secret.

Demon or not, she couldn't stay here and let her soul wither away while Horizon died. She had to do something. She was desperate.

With desperation, come desperate actions. Kara held her blade with trembling hands. She walked up to the Keeper and pointed her blade towards its face. "Tells us how to leave, or it's going to get ugly." She sighed loudly. "I'm not going to ask you again."

The Keeper took a step back, its body twisted in an unnatural way. It lifted its skeletal arms in a plea. "You cannot be serious. I am only a messenger. I do not make the rules. Please put down your weapon."

"I don't care who makes the rules!" Kara moved toward the creature, she wasn't sure what she was about to do, but she had to do something. "You know how to get out of here — tell us! Tell us now, or I'm going to cut you up!" She mimicked the movement with her arm.

The Keeper retreated. It tripped on its own robe, and nearly fell. It caught itself just in time and straightened. "Please! I am no threat. Please don't hurt me. I'm defenseless. I am only the messenger —"

With her anger about to explode, Kara grabbed the Keeper's arm and yanked it forward —

The arm came apart.

Kara stared stupidly at a plastic skeletal arm. It looked like Max, the mascot skeleton from her high school's biology class.

Kara pursed her lips into a thin line. She turned to the Keeper, grabbed a handful of its robe, and kicked it in the stomach.

Two tiny men spilled out from under the cloth. They hit the ground and rolled to a stop. Scrambling, they got to their feet and backed away from Kara, the whites of their eyes showing. They wore simple overalls with white shirts. The taller one had red curly hair that framed his pointy face. The other was balding, with wisps of light brown hair floating off his head. They were middle aged, with neatly trimmed beards. Both were terrified. If Kara hadn't been so angry, she would have laughed. Instead, she growled like an animal.

"What is the meaning of this?" She hissed and threw the robe to the ground. "You better start explaining yourselves … or I will cut your little bodies into tiny little pieces!"

One of the small men flashed his teeth. He rubbed his hands together nervously. "W — we were just having a little fun, that is all. We never dreamed angels could get so … so violent." He forced a smile again. His voice was unnaturally high for a man his age, and Kara was sure this was the one who had done the talking.

"Yes. Please forgive us," said the other man who looked as though he was about to cry. "We get bored you see, and we just wanted to have a little fun. It's just a show."

Kara heard David snort. Kara raised her eyebrows. She wasn't impressed. This was no laughing matter. She stood staring down at the tiny men, irritated to be part of this charade.

"What show? And no more funny business."

"Yes ma'am." Both men bowed at the same time. After a moment, they lifted their arms in the air and shouted. "Okay, boys and girls. Show's over! Pack it up!"

The ground shook beneath Kara's feet and loud noises rang in her ears like cracks of thunder. The fog dissipated. Giant white panels on wheels were pushed away by tiny men and women in denim overalls. The endless heavens of the eighth plane were transformed into a crowded warehouse. Kara recognized the three large smoke machines that were being hauled away. She blinked into massive spotlights. With a click, they turned off. She stood staring around her. This was a set, she realized, with props and smoke machines. This was what the little men had meant by a show. Kara and David had just been part of one. She pursed her lips. It only made her angrier.

"Hey! Wait a minute." Kara went for the little man with the red hair and grabbed his arm. She pulled him around to face her. "For your own good, I'm willing to forget the fact that you just wasted our time with your ridiculous show—but you better tell me the truth now. What is this place? What are we doing here?"

The little man scratched the back of his neck. "Well, it's as we told you before … when we were in character. This *is* the eighth plane. And unfortunately, no one is allowed to leave."

"Not allowed to leave?" David was becoming irritated, too. "Who says? Who's in charge here?" His blues eyes flashed dangerously.

"Orders from the High Council, that is. The archangel Uriel himself," replied the other tiny person in a voice even higher pitched, "says no one is to leave. Too dangerous. Have to stay here."

"Too dangerous? But we *have* to leave. We can't stay here!" Kara's temper flared. Things were just getting worse by the minute. She fought to control her anger. She wanted to strangle the little guy.

"I'm sorry, but you can't. You'll have to sit and wait with the rest of them." The little man turned and pointed in the direction of a large grey panel that covered an entire wall.

Another man waddled over to the panel, put his weight into it, and pushed the panel as it rolled away and folded onto itself. Kara stared at a back room packed with angels. A flashing blue and red neon sign was nailed at the top. It read, *Customer service, now serving angels*. Over a thousand guardian angels sat in small metal chairs. They fidgeted nervously. Kara wondered how long they'd been waiting in that room. She scanned the area for Jenny and Peter. They weren't there. She felt a pressure in her chest and prayed that they had made their way back to Horizon safely.

"You have to take a number and sit with the rest of them." The man rolled up the robe and flung it over his shoulder. "Lilly will take care of you." He skipped away, the black robe dragging on the floor behind him.

Kara turned back and searched the room. A single desk of polished wood stood across the room at the far right. A woman sat in a chair behind the desk. She wore a black vest over a white blouse buttoned all the way to the neck. Her grey hair was pulled back tightly in a bun that rested on the top of her head. Her pointy face was pulled tight, and she wore a deep frown that dragged her forehead down to the bridge of her nose. She reminded Kara of her fourth-grade teacher, Mrs. Wiggins, whose frown and cruel face terrified the children. She suppressed a chill.

To Lilly's right was a large red arrow secured on a tall metal stand with the words, *pick a number*, pointed down. A large roll of numbers spilled to the floor.

David raised his brows. "This is the weirdest day I've ever had as a GA."

"Let's just hope she can tell us how to get back. The longer we waste here, the slimmer our chances are to reach the Legion in time before the demons strike."

David shrugged. "You're right. Well, let's get to it." He strode toward the desk, pushing his way through the tight space. Kara followed him and looked around. She didn't recognize any of the faces. But they all had one thing in common — they were frightened.

David stood before the large red arrow and tore off a number. He stared at it for a moment. He looked up at Kara and handed her the small piece of paper.

Kara seized the ticket. A bell rang, and a number appeared above the arrow: eighty-four. She glanced down at her number, thirty-six thousand seven hundred and ninety-nine. They would be stuck here for days. Kara watched the angel with the number eighty-four walk up to the desk and hand the piece of paper to Lilly. She took the number, crumbled it, and threw it in a waste paper basket behind her without turning her head. Kara thought she looked annoyed.

Kara crumbled her own number and stormed towards the desk. The angel with number eighty-four walked away. Kara took the opportunity, and as the bell rang for the next number she was already standing in front of the desk.

Lilly looked up from under the deep folds of her brows. "Number," she said impatiently and held out her hand. She waited.

Kara caught sight of David standing next to her. She handed Lilly her creased number. She watched the old woman examine the piece of paper. Her eyebrows rose, and the old woman's face twisted in annoyance.

"Can't you read? It says number eighty-five." She pointed to the number above the red arrow with a long crooked finger. "Sit," she ordered, and dismissed Kara with a flick of her hand. Kara clenched her jaw. This was going to be more difficult than she expected.

Kara leaned over the desk, so that the other angels couldn't hear. "Uh … Lilly? Listen, we can't wait here. We have urgent information for the Legion. My partner and I must get to Horizon right now." She hoped she didn't sound too disrespectful. She studied the woman's face for any traces of contempt. There weren't any.

Lilly stared at Kara without blinking. She smiled in amusement. "Do you have number eighty-five?"

"No, but—"

"Then sit down!"

Kara flinched. How dare this woman speak to her like this? She clenched her trembling fingers into fists. She wanted to punch her. She slammed her hand on the desk. The boom echoed louder throughout the room than she would have wanted. All the GAs were listening in.

"Listen, lady," hissed Kara, and she noticed David take a step back. "I don't have time for your attitude and stupidity!" Her voice carried through the room. "If you don't let us get back, the Legion will be destroyed! And it'll be because of you!" She pointed her finger inches from Lilly's face. That seemed to anger the woman.

Lilly looked as though she had bitten into something bitter. Her eyes became tight slits and Kara could hardly see the green in them anymore.

Lilly pushed back her chair and stood up. "Listen to me carefully, guardian. As I have been explaining for the last five hours to the rest of your kin—," she waved her skinny arm in the direction of the angels sitting in the chairs, "you cannot go back to Horizon. Something has broken the veil. All angels trying to get back to Horizon from Earth will land here. The High Council has instructed us to keep you here safely until they fix the problem. So you see, you cannot go anywhere ... no matter how much you raise your voice to me."

Kara glared down at the tiny woman. "This is exactly why we must go."

Kara tried to calm the shaking in her voice. "There are things you don't know ... don't understand. Terrible things will happen if we don't get in touch with the Legion in time, you must believe us — "

"What things?" Lilly crossed her arms over her chest. "What things, guardian?" she repeated, a hint of concern in her commanding voice.

Kara wondered if she should tell this old fool. She decided that she would and hoped she would understand. "Asmodeus is planning an attack on Horizon. He used the attacks on the mortal world as a diversion. We know it to be true. He's also probably causing this disruption in the veil."

"With all the angels gone to save mortal souls, plus the ones stuck here — he has a great chance of succeeding."

David stood by Kara. "This is very serious, Lilly." David put on the charm. "We're not here to get you into any kind of trouble, I promise. We just need you to help us get back."

The old woman stood motionless, her cold stare fixed on them both. For the moment no one spoke.

"If we can't get through to Horizon ... then at least let us send them a message," pleaded David.

"You can't," said Lilly through gritted teeth. "That's not possible."

"Surely you can communicate with them? You just said they gave you orders to keep everyone here — "

"No, as I said ... it's not possible."

"Why not?" Kara heard the anger in David's voice. He too was losing his patience with the old woman.

Lilly studied their faces for a minute. Her green eyes focused on Kara. "You are the angel, Kara? Aren't you?"

"Yes." Kara was running out of patience and time.

Lilly fell back into her seat, and Kara thought she had paled. "If what you say is true, then it is grave indeed. I had wondered why we had lost all communication with Horizon. They can't hear us anymore. We are unable to communicate with them. No messages can get through anymore."

Kara's eyes were level with Lilly's. "Then let us through, let us get back."

The old woman stared into space. She looked up at the two of them and shook her head. "It is too dangerous. Your angel bodies will die. I cannot be responsible for your deaths."

Kara pressed her hands on the desk. "If you don't let us go, you'll be responsible for a lot more than just two deaths."

Lilly shook her head again. She looked at them with sad eyes. "You don't understand. With the veil broken, it is too dangerous to travel back to Horizon. Your supernatural bodies will burn and fall apart. Without vega, your bodies will disintegrate into nothingness. You will die ... the true death."

Kara refused to believe it. They hadn't gone through all this mess to be told they couldn't reach Horizon. "Is there a chance that we might not? Is there a chance we might survive?"

Lilly didn't answer. She only stared at her.

"Well, is there?"

The old woman closed her eyes. "Yes. There is a slight chance. A very slight chance you might survive —"

"So we'll do it. We'll take that chance."

Lilly stared at Kara, bewildered for a long moment. After a while she relaxed. She seemed to have accepted Kara's request. She stood up and called out.

"Rosy! I need you to replace me for fifteen minutes."

A plump young woman with a tan skirt suit pushed her way through the crowd. Her curly blond hair bounced from her shoulders as she went to busy herself with the angel customers. Lilly made her way around her desk and gestured for Kara and David to follow her.

She led them out of the room and across the warehouse towards the back. They followed her through a small corridor and down a few steps leading to a bottom level. Kara couldn't see anything through the darkness. Lilly climbed up a ladder and flicked a switch. Immediately the room was bathed in a soft yellow light. A large elevator shaft rose against the back wall. A metal gate was secured before it. Kara heard a tinkle, and saw Lilly pull out a large set of keys. She waddled over to the large elevator and stood up on her toes. She jammed a key into an iron key hole and turned—

The ground shook as light exploded from the key hole. The elevator was illuminated in a blue light. Blue shards of light coiled around the elevator and went out. The room stood still once again.

David smiled. "Wow. What kind of elevator is this?" He walked across the room and dragged his hand against the metal gate. "It looks ancient."

"That's because it is." Lilly grabbed hold of the gate and with great effort, she pulled it across. Two solid metal doors stood before them. "This elevator was one of the first built by the archangels, thousands of years ago. They stopped using it because it had some defects. Angels would come back missing arms and legs. It became too dangerous to let anyone use it. They then designed the EL20 models—the ones you've used, and forgot about this one. It hasn't been used in over five hundred years. It's kept only for emergencies. I don't even know if it'll work."

Kara pressed her hand against the doors. It was cool. "Well, this is definitely an emergency—"

The doors creaked, and slid open. Kara jumped back in alarm.

Beyond the doors was a large compartment. The walls were metal and the floor was crooked slabs of concrete. It wasn't nearly as fancy as the elevators Kara was used to. But this wasn't the time to get picky. Kara made up her mind and stepped into the elevator. David stepped in beside her. She looked around. Smooth metal walls surrounded them. There were no buttons anywhere. Kara thought it strange that there was no control panel.

Lilly grabbed the metal gate and pulled it across them on the other side. She stepped back and watched them with a worried expression.

"How do we know where the elevator is going?" asked Kara, with her hand on the wall where the control panel ought to be.

Lilly forced a smile. "You don't. If you survive the journey, it'll take you to Horizon. But where, is beyond me."

"Great," mumbled Kara.

"Safe journey back. Best of luck." She leaned over and pressed her finger on a panel on the exterior wall.

With a loud screeching noise the doors jerked and slid slowly across the front. David squeezed her hand in his. She looked into his blue eyes and returned his squeeze. David was as terrified as she was.

The elevator jerked to life. She felt pressure pulling her in every direction. The pulling increased, and she felt as though her body would rip apart. She hung onto David desperately. What have they gotten themselves into? David's body shook, and she felt hers move. Kara yelled in surprise. David's body suddenly disappeared. It reappeared a second later, but it was transparent. She could see the metal wall through him, as though she was looking through a heat wave. She looked down. Her lower body and legs were a white mist. Was this the end? Another wave of pain attacked. Kara let out a cry. She shook uncontrollably. She felt as though she was in a blender. She knew her body was breaking. They were going to die.

She looked at David's body. She had to concentrate hard to see him. He was almost completely invisible. She could make out pain on his face. Suddenly, miniscule pieces of his body started to detach themselves. He was coming apart. Panicked, Kara pressed her body against his, hoping to hold him together. Her arms were breaking apart too. Kara shook. She wouldn't let them die.

Kara used the only power she had left. She let all her anger flare inside her. She felt the elemental power answering her call. She willed it forward, and grasped it. Her vision exploded in golden hues. A golden light danced at the tip of her fingers. She gently pressed against David's shoulders and golden beams coiled in and around them as they stood. Soon their bodies radiated a brilliant golden color. She could finally see David's face more clearly. He was frightened, but he managed a smile. Kara thought he looked beautiful highlighted in gold. Her plan seemed to be working. Their bodies were staying intact.

There was a sudden loud crack. Kara and David were thrown to the ground. The bond with the elemental power was broken. Kara sensed the elevator had stopped moving. She pushed herself up on her elbows as the doors slid open.

Loud wails sounded all around them. Blasts of red and white illuminated the sky. The smell of smoke entered the elevator. Kara blinked through a heavy grey haze. The vast desert in Operations was in flames. The tents were on fire. Sounds of battle were everywhere.

The war had already begun. They were too late.

Chapter 13
A War of Angels

"Kara! Let's move!"

But Kara's body wouldn't budge. She stood frozen in place, staring out onto a massacre. The normal blue skies of Operations were dark and covered in a grey haze of smoke. Flickering embers rained down from the skies and blanketed the desert in a blanket of flames. Everywhere she looked angels were being ripped to pieces, their bodies evaporating into showers of brilliant crystals. A thunderous boom resonated around them. Black lightning from the sky hit several angels. Their bodies exploded and were swept away in the fiery sand storm.

"Kara!" David pulled Kara out of the elevator by force. She snapped out of her frozen trance and stumbled along. A deafening crash shook the ground. Kara felt a sudden sharp pain at her side. She fell to her knees and turned around. A mountain of concrete ruble was all that was left of the monumental elevator. Fire and smoke rose in streaks from its broken shell.

David pulled Kara to her feet and dragged her with him in a run. Powerful winds slapped her face. A flurry of sand scratched her eyes. Kara made her eyes into slits and tried to see through the oncoming sand storm. Her foot caught on something, and she nearly fell. She regained her balance and looked at what made her trip. The fur of a dead chimpanzee who had been covered in blankets of sand rippled in the strong winds. She recognized his face — Chimp 5M51. She wanted to scream.

After a moment, she felt David's presence beside her. He looked horrified. She followed his gaze.

Out in the distance, piles of metal and wood sprouted from the desert like fractured bones from a ruptured abdomen. Remnants of the elevators and their operators were spread out for miles. Some were ablaze, while others lay in silent piles of rubble. She understood now why they couldn't access Horizon as they had before. The demons had destroyed the elevators and killed the operators. Then she caught a glimpse of some terrified black and brown primates hiding behind boulders. She prayed the demons would overlook them.

A distant laugh caught Kara's attention. She looked up into the darkened skies. Massive wings cut through clouds of smoke and beat the skies above her. A two-legged creature with a long snake-like body and reptilian head banked easily through the clouds. A long, sharply pointed tail rippled behind it. Its body was covered in yellow and red flames, and somehow Kara could see through it. The demon swooped towards the battlefield. It glided through clouds of smoke and dove suddenly towards a group of guardians. A figure was riding the demon. His wicked laugh caused a chill to roll up Kara's spine. She recognized

Asmodeus. He sat upon the beast, his blood-red suit rippled in the wind. His arms were raised in the air. Black lighting from his hands struck the angels below. Kara knew they didn't stand a chance. He was merciless. With a sharp popping sound, their bodies exploded in a blur of white dust.

Asmodeus roared in laughter. She watched him raise his arms again. Black electricity blasted out of his hands and struck the ground. A tremor passed under Kara's feet. The ground shook and the desert was split by a crevice that extended out of sight beyond the red hills.

Kara couldn't see a bottom, and she watched in horror as hundreds of angels fell wailing down into the abyss.

David pulled her into a run with him. Kara held on tightly to David's hand, afraid to let go. His soul blade was brandished in front of him.

A shadow covered the ground — the eagles. The guardians of Tartarus dove through the blackened skies like missiles. They ploughed through a horde of demons and ripped them apart easily with their razor sharp talons. Demons wailed as the eagles tore out their innards and crushed their skulls with their feet.

A massive demon with large fly-like wings charged at the eagles. It grabbed one by the neck with its large maw. Kara heard a snap. The eagle fell limply to the ground. More insect-like demons took to the skies and launched another attack. Large golden feathers rained down on Kara and David as the eagles wrestled against the new breeds from the Netherworld. The sky was alive with the horrifying sounds of flesh being ripped apart. Kara feared for the eagles.

"Kara, we have to move! We can't stay here." David yelled over the howling winds and the wails of the eagles and demons.

Kara wiped the hair from her eyes. "I know ... but where are we going?"

"I don't know. Let's keep moving until we find someplace safe. We're going to get killed if we stay here. Come on—" David urged her on.

Kara's feet sank into the red sand as she sprinted down a gully behind David. The sounds of battle blasted into their ears from every direction as they ran, urging them on. The horror of it all pained her. She had failed to warn the Legion before the attacks. What would happen to them?

A fleet of guardians appeared before them a hundred feet away. They formed a strong line above a rise. Forty sturdy men and women, all clad in armor, waited to do battle. Their long silver swords and daggers hung at their sides. Kara saw bows strapped across a few of the women's shoulders. Some also carried glowing red and white orbs in their hands. Kara immediately recognized them as the firestones and moonstones. They showed no fear. These were the real warriors, Kara told herself. They were ageless, experienced soldiers ready to fight till the true death.

Movement caught Kara's eye. She turned.

Ten higher demons walked casually in the red sand. Their identical faces bore no expression. Black smoke coiled around their death blades and rose around their arms. Kara found it strange how clean their grey suits appeared, considering the dirt and smoke everywhere. Their clothes showed no traces of a struggle.

The demons reached the bottom of the hill. Kara heard someone call out an order, and the angels' line broke in half. She watched as the guardians stormed down to meet the higher demons head on. A young guardian about her age ran with her blade held out before her. Long red hair spilled out behind her as she ran. She launched herself at the nearest demon. With her arm held high, she leaped into the air and brought her blade down in a long curving arc, aimed at his neck. Kara was sure she had him. There was a sudden blur, and the young woman screamed. Kara caught a glimpse of a blade landing in the sand. The higher demon's blade was impaled in her abdomen. With a flash, he forced the blade down like cutting through a loaf of bread, and pulled her apart with his hands, as though she was nothing but paper. Her body plopped to the floor in two severed pieces. Kara watched in horror as the demon crouched down and ingested the angel's soul. It shivered in delight as it rose.

The murder of their fellow soldier didn't slow down the rest of the fleet. They attacked hard, and with everything they had. Screams and the sounds of metal hitting metal rose up around them. A soul blade punctured the back of an unsuspecting higher demon. It cried out and reached behind its back trying to free itself from the pain. With its attention disrupted momentarily, another angel skewered it with its blade, followed by another, and then another. Finally, the higher demon fell to its knees. It smiled. It took its own blade and slashed it across its neck. The body rose up in black flames and soon disintegrated into a pile of dust which the wind blew away. Kara had never seen a higher demon die before. She felt satisfied and disgusted at the same time. But that was the only one. The remaining nine had killed the guardians. Their bodies were spread out on the ground, soulless and empty.

Kara heard another battle cry. The last of the angels charged. Kara winced at how easily they lost their lives. The angels fought back with everything they had, but they were no match for the higher demons. She had to do something. She felt herself lean forward —

"What do you think you're doing?" David pulled Kara towards him. "You can't do anything for them now. It's too late. We have to get out of here!"

Kara shook her head and tried to pull free from David's iron grip. "I have to! This is my fault. I have to save them! I can't just stand here and watch while they all get killed. Let me go!"

"No. It's suicide. I won't let you!"

Kara's anger flared inside her. "Let go of me, David!"

She yanked her arm free. "We have to do something!"

Before David knew what she was doing, Kara pushed him hard and stole his soul blade. She ran before he could stop her. She heard him call out her name a few times, but then his voice was lost in the sounds of battle.

She let her fury loose, recalling all the deaths of the innocent mortals and angels. *Come*, urged Kara. She felt the tingle of power scurrying through her. She felt it come alive and surge down to her finger tips. It wrapped around her like a warm blanket. Kara embraced it. She felt the wild elemental energy fueling itself on her hatred for what the demons had done to Horizon, and on her hatred of what Asmodeus had done to her.

A demon nearby severed a guardian's head and laughed as it kicked it like a ball. Kara rushed towards the demon, her blade ready, and her elemental's golden power dancing on her finger tips. She reached out—

A sting exploded in her back. Pain was immediate and overwhelming. She cried out and tumbled to the ground on her knees.

Laughs echoed all around her.

She reached behind her and felt three handles. She knew instantly that they were death blades. Her hand burned as she wrapped it around a handle and pulled it free from her back. She tossed the blade and reached out for another—

Something kicked her in the face. Kara went sprawling to the ground. She could feel the blades' poison spread through her, eating at her core like acid. Black vapors coiled around her body. She had to get them out soon or she would die.

"Well, well, well. What do we have here?"

Kara blinked through a gust of sand. A higher demon stood above her. Its white skin wrinkled into a devilish grin. Its black bottomless eyes mocked her.

"Thought you could use that power of yours, did you?"

The higher demon laughed, and Kara cursed her own stupidity.

"I think it's time to put an end to the famous Kara Nightingale. My lord has had enough of your ... interruptions. You cannot escape from your true death, my dear. Your special powers cannot save you now."

The demon drew another death blade. He licked the blade and grinned. In a flash, he threw the blade towards Kara's face —

Something silver caught the death blade in midair and deflected it to the side. Another flash of silver and a series of sharp noises — she heard a scream, and a silver blade punctured through the back of the demon's head and came out through its eye socket.

A figure in black flew over Kara and landed before the wailing demon. With one strike, the figure beheaded the demon. Kara watched as the head hit the ground with a thump. The demon's body went up in black flames as the other demon's had, and it dissolved into a cloud of black dust.

Kara felt a pressure on her back, and then a release. She knew instantly the blades had been removed. She rolled over.

The figure behind her was slightly built and dressed like a CDD field agent with black pants and top. Kara figured she was female. Soul blades were secured in leather sheaths tied around her thighs and ankles. Her long black hair was pulled back into a tight braid.

The guardian turned around and kneeled before Kara. She spoke with concern and urgency.

"Kara! What are you doing here? You're supposed to be on the 8th plane and safe."

Kara couldn't speak.

She stared into big brown eyes like her own. Even wrinkled in worry, the face was smooth and uncommonly beautiful. Her naturally red lips were pursed tight.

Finally, Kara found her voice.

"Mom?"

CHAPTER 14
ON THE MOVE

"**M**om!" Kara screamed. She jumped to her feet and wrapped her arms around her mother.

Her mother squeezed back, but released Kara gently. "Kara, how did you get through? The demons destroyed the elevators — the connections are lost — any chance of traveling back and forth from the mortal world is impossible. How is it that you are standing here?"

Kara's mother looked over her shoulder nervously. They couldn't stand here for much longer.

"We took an elevator from the eighth plane." By her mother's bewildered expression Kara knew she had to explain a little further. "It was an old elevator, a really old one — built thousands of years ago. And Lilly let us use it to get here."

Her mother shook her head. "But your bodies would have been ripped apart? It's impossible —"

"It was a risk, we knew, but we were determined to warn the Legion. We figured out what Asmodeus was planning ... part of what's happening is *my* fault. I had to warn the Legion."

"But how, Kara? How are you responsible for this?"

Kara looked at her boots. "I'm not like you and the others, mom. I'm different. And I used that part that's different." She looked up and met her mother's eyes. "I used my *elemental* part to keep us together on the elevator. It worked."

"Who's us? Who's with you?" Kara's mother looked over her shoulder again.

Kara sighed. "My friend David. He was with me when we landed in the eighth plane. We came here together."

"That was reckless, Kara," said her mother, her voice suddenly hard. "You could have died ... and David too."

Kara looked at her fingers. "I know. But we didn't. We thought we had enough time to get to Horizon before the attacks started ... guess we were wrong."

"It's okay, my darling girl," said her mother gently. "You did what you did because you felt it was the right thing to do. It was crazy — but I understand why you did it. I probably would have done the same."

Kara gazed into her mother's face. She felt so many emotions at once. Her mother's soul had survived. She was safe, and standing before her as a guardian angel. Questions filled her mind. She wanted to know about her mother's life as a guardian, how it felt. But mostly, Kara wanted to know how her mother could have fallen in love with Asmodeus.

"Mom ... how could you fall —"

"Kara!" David rushed towards them. "Are you crazy? What's the matter with you?" He pushed himself between them.

His voice was loud with anger, but his eyes were soft with concern. "You could have been killed!" His face was inches from Kara's. Her mother raised her eyebrows and looked over at Kara with the hint of a smile on her lips.

Kara took a step back and raised her arms. "Well, I'm fine, as you see. Thanks to Danielle, my mother."

"Your mother?" David stared open-mouthed at Kara's mother. His eyes moved up and down, inspecting every inch of her body. At last, David raised an eyebrow. "You never told me she was a babe — ow!"

Kara's mother grabbed them both by the elbows and turned them towards her.

"Now listen, both of you. We can't stay here. We're sitting ducks if we stay in Operations." She looked over her shoulder and spoke with more urgency. "Michael and Gabriel have moved what remains of the Legion to level three, Miracles Division. The demons haven't been able to break through the mountain ... for the moment. But it won't last forever. For the time being, it's headquarters. Missions are being deployed from there. I'll explain things more in detail once we're safe."

Danielle passed soul blades to both of them. "Take these. Let's go kids."

Kara watched her mother sprint over flaming debris and ran to catch up to her. For a woman in her early forties, she moved faster than Kara and David. Goes to show that mortality has no effect in Horizon, Kara thought to herself. Age has no meaning here.

The trio ran side by side, up and down the sandy slopes. The skies had become darker. Black clouds raced across the remaining grey sky, sucking out the light. Soon all would be consumed in darkness. Kara wondered if her mother knew where she was leading them. From what Kara could see between the sand and the ashes, there were only more rolling hills ahead of them and out into the distance.

A deafening wail rose up around them. Danielle lifted her hand and motioned for them to lie low. Kara kneeled beside her mother. She felt David on her right. Kara peered out into the dark desert. A twister of sand and ashes rolled across the dunes. She couldn't see beyond the thick windstorm.

A shadow moved about two hundred feet in front of them. Kara strained to see. The thing was massive and low to the ground. The creature squatted and tilted its head, as if it were following a scent in the air. Its four legs carried a body covered in sharp spikes from head to tail. It took no heed of the three of them as it scuttled on. Grunts escaped the creature, low at first, and then it howled. Suddenly the demon charged. Kara lifted her head to see what the demon was about to assault. Her throat tightened. An elevator shaft stood above a mound of sand with its doors open. The operator cowered in a corner. He covered his head with his hands. Kara could see him shaking with fear. The demon galloped towards him, slashing at the ground as it ran.

Kara stood up—

Suddenly, a beam of white light flared and caught the demon in the chest. The creature wailed and was thrown back a hundred feet. It landed hard on the ground and skidded to a stop, its body coated in red sand. After a second, the creature struggled to its feet. Its body sizzled and popped, and Kara saw scorched flesh fall to the ground. The wind carried the smell of burnt flesh. The demon limped towards the elevator. It opened its large maw in an angry roar.

Another beam of light hit the demon. The creature was hoisted in the air and hovered for a moment. A cry escaped the creature as it fell limply to the ground. It didn't move again.

"Take that, you beast!" An oracle rolled into view. His giant crystal blazed in white flames, illuminating the oracle and the sand around him in a circle of bright light. He stood on his crystal ball, hands on his hips. He raised his fist. "There's plenty more where that came from!"

"Come on." Danielle led Kara and David towards the elevator. The oracle spotted them, and rolled his crystal ball with his feet to meet them. He looked relieved to see them.

"Thank you, oracle," said Danielle. She bowed her head slightly. Her long braid rolled off her back and dangled by the side of her face. "You have no idea how much you've helped. Without this elevator, we can't reach the other levels. I think this may be one of the last working elevators."

The oracle seemed pleased with the compliment. "We oracles might be ancient, but there's still a fighter in each of us. We won't let our world be infected by filthy demons." He rolled his beard around his fingers nervously.

"Kara...David...quickly now." Danielle shot a quick glance around the desert before hopping inside the elevator. "There's not much time. We must go. Now!"

Kara thanked the oracle and followed her mother inside the elevator. She leaned against the polished wood panels, her mind racing. A musty smell lingered in the air, just as she remembered. David pressed his back against the back panel next to her. Their eyes met. David gave her a reassuring smile. Kara didn't smile back.

"Level three, please. Miracles Division, and hurry," called Danielle.

Kara heard a whimper and looked down. The elevator's operator was huddled into a tight ball near the bottom right corner of the control panel. His black fur glistened as he shivered. He looked up at her. His brown eyes were wide and wet. Kara heard clinking sounds, and she realized it came from his chattering teeth. The poor creature was terrified. He reminded her of chimp 5M51, only slightly smaller. Before she knew what she was doing, she knelt down beside him. She reached out and stroked him gently on the arm.

"You're safe now. It's going to be okay. What's your name?"

She felt sorry for the chimp. No creature deserved this, especially the primates. They weren't trained fighters. This was unknown territory to them. "We need for you to be strong now. We need to get to level three. Can you do that for us?" She knew she could just press the button herself, but helping this poor creature made her feel better, even if it was briefly.

The chimp blinked up at Kara. And for a while, he didn't move. And then he spoke. "Ch—chimp 2M24." Slowly, the chimp rose to his feet. He stood about as tall as Kara's middle. Although still shaking, he looked more in control of his fears. He lifted a shaking finger, and pressed the number three button on the control panel.

"Level three! Miracles Division," said the chimp. The doors slid shut. Chimp 2M24 slumped against the wall, relieved.

With a jolt, the elevator came to life. Kara felt pressure on her head and shoulders as they lifted to a higher level. She wondered what to expect once the doors opened. Would they be in the heart of another battle?

There was a sudden violent jerk, and Kara and the others were thrown against the opposite wall. Kara reached out and held on to David. She feared they wouldn't make it to the next level. Surprisingly, the doors opened, and Kara stared out onto a beautiful lush green valley.

Danielle was the first one out, followed by David. Kara stood by the door and looked down at the chimp. He was still shivering, but he looked more composed. Kara thanked him and jumped out.

"Let's hurry. We don't know what lurks in the forest." Danielle drew out a blade. It gleamed in the sun and reflected golden streaks on her face. "Many have died protecting the mountain. We can't linger here. Come on."

Kara and David exchanged a look and took off after her.

Miracles Division was just as beautiful as Kara remembered. She looked up into the scarlet and orange sky that topped the thick forest. A light breeze carried the smell of pine trees and damp earth. Something caught her eye. A guardian leaned against a large tree, his body hidden in the shadows. He gave a nod as they rushed passed him. Kara noticed many others, well hidden in the dense forest. They wore long green cloaks, and Kara thought they looked like wood elves.

Kara followed the others up a dirt path. Soon the forest cleared, and she looked out across a valley to a mountain that rose high above and was lost in the clouds. At a run, they reached the base of the mountain within minutes. Black marks scorched the stone walls of the buildings that lined the main entry. Smoke coiled up and around the front. A large group of oracles and guardian angels poured water on small fires around the base of the buildings.

Danielle led them through a jungle of winding and turning walkways to a large wooden door. She pushed it open and walked through. They stood on the threshold of a large chamber.

Sunlight spilled through square openings at the top. Kara recognized it instantly as one of the many healing chambers. A dozen guardian angels in blue lab coats worked feverishly mixing and measuring elements in glass containers. There was a sudden cry of alarm. One of the guardians ran past Kara holding up a glass bottle of orange liquid and dashed out the door. It looked a lot like the orange sticky substance from the Healing-Xpress.

Two exceptionally large men sat at a wooden table at the far end of the chamber. Their heads were bent in conversation and a bundle wrapped in a shiny golden cloth lay on the table. They pushed back their chairs and stood as the group entered. Kara recognized them immediately. The archangel Michael stood a head taller than Gabriel; his silky brown hair framed his perfectly chiseled face. He wore a silver and golden robe that hung snuggly around his muscular shoulders. He looked puzzled. Clearly he felt like her mother — Kara and David weren't supposed to be here. His hazel eyes were fixed upon Kara. She looked away.

A beautiful Asian-looking woman, draped in white linen with jet-black hair that spilled all the way down her back, rushed towards them with her arms outstretched.

"Kara! David! What in the souls are you doing here?" The archangel Raphael grabbed David and Kara and squeezed them tightly against her. Kara was sure David was enjoying this. He always acted strangely when the stunning Raphael was in the same room. Finally she let them go. Kara noticed a stupid grin on David's face. "I have no idea how you managed to get here, but I'm very happy to see you both safe … and in one piece."

"Well, you know me, I'm indestructible." David raked his hair with his fingers—his attempt at flirting made Kara want to gag.

Raphael laughed softly. "Yes, but always getting into trouble. Well, I'm glad you two are safe with me now."

"I always feel safe when I'm around you …" David's blue eyes sparkled.

Kara rolled her eyes and wished David would stop embarrassing himself. Her mother smiled at her. Kara sighed and squeezed her mother in a tight hug.

Her mother kissed the top of her head. "I'm so happy you're safe. I was so worried."

Kara buried her face into her mother's shoulder. "I missed you, mom."

Danielle rubbed her daughter's back. "I missed you too, Kara. I wish I could have been there for you. You must have been terrified with all this supernatural stuff … about who you are … of how special you are. After Raphael brought me back, she told me everything you did for me—and for the Legion." She pushed Kara back gently. "I'm so proud of you, my beautiful daughter."

Kara wished she could cry, but settled on being held by her mother. She hadn't realized how much she missed her. Kara hung her head. "I'm sorry I never believed your stories about demons, mom. You have no idea how sorry."

Her mother laughed. Kara had forgotten how much she loved her mother's laugh. "Don't worry about that. How could you? I didn't know you were chosen, like me. Had I known, things would have been different, let me tell ya. But the Legion only gave me back a few memories at a time after each mission. It's no wonder you thought your mother was nuts. I thought I was nuts. I just wished I could have been there for you, when things got … complicated."

Kara smiled. Her mother always made her feel better. Something occurred to her. "Mom … about my father —"

The door to the chamber burst open, and a woman collapsed to the floor. Her curly red hair was a tangled mess and covered most of her face. Her green robes were torn and covered in dust. Bright light escaped from her many wounds. She wasn't moving.

"Camael!" Raphael rushed to the woman's aid. She held her to her breast and wiped the hair from her face. "Camael! What happened? Who did this to you?"

The archangel struggled to open her mouth. Her lips trembled as she strained to form the words.

"Asmodeus … killed Uriel. He has conquered the High Council."

CHAPTER 15
INFERNO

Kara watched helplessly as Michael and Raphael carried the archangel Camael to one of the wooden tables. Raphael folded a bundle of cloth hastily and used it as a pillow. She took Camael's hands and placed them at her side, whispering to her softly. Her wounds were severe, and Kara wondered if she would survive.

She watched silently as Raphael pressed her hands together in front of her and closed her eyes. As if in prayer, she stood there for a moment without moving. Her skin gave off a soft white glow.

Raphael opened her eyes suddenly. They had become glowing white spheres. She stared down at the injured archangel, with eyes like tiny suns. With open palms, she placed her hands on Camael's chest. Rays of light poured from her touch, and enveloped Camael's body in a coverlet of white light. Kara watched as Camael's body absorbed the light like a sponge. After a moment, the lesions on Camael's body grew smaller until the skin sealed itself. Soon every last cut was mended. Raphael helped Camael to a sitting position and kept her arm wrapped around her shoulders. Her face still held traces of agony, but otherwise Kara thought she looked well enough. She sighed in relief.

"She'll be fine, Raphael is an incredible healer," said her mother.

"Asmodeus is a monster. He can't get away with this — with everything he's done." Kara's voice rose unintentionally, and she lowered it when she saw the grave expression on her mother's face.

Kara's mother gave her a weak smile and spoke to her softly so that only she could hear. "About your father ... I've been told you know who he is."

Kara stared into her mother's big brown eyes. Sadness reflected in them. "Mom ... when you met him, couldn't you tell he was a demon?"

Her mother shook her head. "I didn't know he was a demon. If I had known ... I would never have married him. How could I? I was in my mortal body when I met him the first time. He was tall and so handsome. He told me his name was Samuel. I fell in love with him that very first day — don't look at me like that — he was good to me, Kara — and to you, too. He wasn't this evil thing that he has become. I believe he wasn't always evil ... he changed."

"And not in a good way. He's evil, mom. The worse kind of evil you can imagine."

Her mother twitched uncomfortably. "I know. And it's hard to believe I ever felt anything for someone so cruel."

"And being a guardian, couldn't you tell he was a demon? Couldn't you see demons back when you were a mortal? Why couldn't you see through him, mom?"

"It wasn't like that. I never saw demons when we were together. I only saw him as a mortal man, with mortal flesh. And then I got pregnant with you, we were happy. And then five years later ... he died suddenly ... well, his mortal suit died. I had no idea that he had been planning this all along, Kara — believe me. Then a few months ago, I was in the kitchen and three higher demons attacked me. I don't remember anything else after that."

Kara put her hand on her mom's shoulder tenderly. "It's okay, mom. I get it."

"The last thing I do remember is waking up in the Healing-Xpress. Raphael had a towel ready, and she told me everything. She told me who Samuel really was, and how he had used me. She also told me that you were a guardian, too, but with a special talent. After she explained about your elemental power, I was terrified for you. This *elemental* power is dangerous. I'm so angry at what he's done to you." Danielle embraced her daughter. "I'm so sorry, Kara. If I could take it all away for you, and give you a normal life ... I would."

"I know, mom. It's not your fault. You didn't know. Besides, I like being a guardian. It has its moments." Kara laughed softly into her mother's shoulder. "I just wished I could have stopped this somehow. Stopped the killings."

"Don't worry. The Legion is stronger than you think. We will survive this."

Kara hoped her mother was right. She felt a presence behind her, and looked up to see Michael approaching the table. He hovered above the injured archangel. He took Camael's hand in his gently. His beautiful face was transformed into something terrifying, almost feral. His eyes were wild. Kara felt suddenly cold. But when he spoke his voice was gentle. "Camael. Can you tell us what happened?"

The archangel Camael stared at the table for a moment before answering.

"It happened so fast." She shook her head. "We never imagined the High Council could be under attack—never. We weren't prepared." She stared at her trembling hands, and wrapped them into tight fists. Kara wanted to reach out to her and comfort her, but she feared what Michael would do. Perhaps it wasn't her place. So she took a step forward instead.

"Do not fret, Camael. You cannot blame yourself for what happened," said Michael, his voice was full of compassion. He pressed his hand over hers kindly.

"The doors burst open," continued Camael, her voice wavering. "So many of them … so many of them." Her eyes were filled with terror. Her body shook uncontrollably. Kara wondered if she had gone mad with what she'd witnessed. She wouldn't blame her if she had.

Michael squeezed her hand tenderly. "It's okay. You're safe now. Please, Camael—tell us what happened, it's very important. Don't be afraid."

Kara and the rest of the team waited patiently as the archangel composed herself and started her story once again.

"We were taken by surprise. At first, hoards of lower demons ravaged the chamber, destroying everything. Then the higher demons came." Camael stared into space. "And then ... he came."

"Asmodeus," said Michael.

"Yes." Camael raised her head and met Michael's eyes. "He just started killing council members—ripping them apart. Their screams ... their screams." She covered her ears with her hands and shook her head.

"He drank in their essences, Michael! Like a beast! How could he have done that? He took their life forces into himself and strutted around the chamber laughing. Uriel tried to stop him. He really tried. He was the strongest of us. But Asmodeus just laughed at him. He mocked him, and then he ... he killed him. He killed Uriel!" Camael screamed his name and collapsed into Raphael's arms.

Kara felt numb. Uriel was dead. Asmodeus had killed him. It was unreal that someone so powerful could be gone. He had been kind to her at times. Her soul mourned his loss.

Camael pulled Michael closer to her. "He tortured him, Michael! Tortured him! They held him down and cut off pieces slowly. Asmodeus laughed and danced as Uriel cried out in pain. It was horrible. He took his essence, and then came after me. I ... I thought I was going to be the next." She closed her eyes. "He hurt me. It—burned. I wanted the pain to stop. I wanted to die. But then he stopped. He said he wanted me to get out ... to deliver a message to you."

"What's the message?"

"That it's over. The Legion has lost." Camael opened her eyes and terror flashed across her face. "To join him now ... or die. He said he would gladly fight you."

Michael let go of Camael. "If it's a fight he wants, then a fight he shall have. He will taste the bitterness of true death. He will die at the hands of an inferno blade."

Michael's silver and gold robes rippled out behind him as he crossed the chamber. He stood before the parcel wrapped in golden cloth. Kara watched as Gabriel eyed it suspiciously. She shifted her weight nervously. What was wrapped in that piece of cloth? And what exactly was an inferno? The tension was driving her nuts.

After a moment, Michael reached out and removed the cloth. Kara gasped. Flames rose from the spot where the item lay. And for a moment, the table was bathed in a soft golden color. Kara crossed the room. She could see yellow flames reflected in Michael's eyes. She looked down. A single golden dagger rested above a piece of cloth. Flames flickered and danced around the handle and around the blade. The blade shimmered. It was a blade made of fire.

Michael lifted the dagger in the air. Golden flames wrapped around his hand and spilled towards his arms. His entire arm was aflame in golden fire. With his face tightly determined, he looked taller and more fearsome. Kara wondered if that was an after effect of the blade. He looked terrifying. She realized she was more fearful of him, than any demon. Kara felt herself stepping back. If anyone could defeat Asmodeus, she was certain it would be Michael.

Michael lowered his arm and examined the blade more closely. "A weapon built by the creators from the flames of the heavens, for one purpose only—to bring the true death to an archangel. The blade that kills archangels will eliminate the demon Asmodeus."

Kara watched the fire licking around Michael's hands and down his arms. It came as no surprise now why Gabriel had eyed it with a reproachful glare. He knew it could kill him.

"Wait!" Camael threw her arms in the air. "You don't know what he's done. You don't understand the power he has now —"

"No archangel can survive the strike of the inferno. He will die."

Camael shook her head. "I don't think ... you don't understand. He's not just a demon anymore. He's changed."

Raphael exchanged a look of concern with Michael, but he ignored it. She brushed a long lock of hair from Camael's face. "What do you mean, Camael? In what way has he changed?"

Camael struggled with what she was about to say. "He has *ingested* the souls of archangels. Their energy flows inside him. Their strength—is now *his* strength. He will not be easily defeated."

"He *will* be defeated, nonetheless." Michael's eyes blazed with hatred.

"He has been planning this for a very long time. He's always wanted to control Horizon—"

"He has?" blurted Kara before she could control herself. All eyes were on her, and she wished she could disappear.

Camael turned and regarded Kara for a moment. Her voice was calm when she spoke. "Yes. Even as an archangel, I could see his lust for power, and it worried me. His soul slowly corrupted itself. His charm and his natural ability to lead created a following. Angels and archangels alike listened to and adored him. It was too easy for him, and his hunger for power grew. He contemplated a takeover with a group of our most powerful and talented angels. He nearly succeeded, you know. But in the end, he didn't have enough members, and the Legion vanquished them. Asmodeus and his followers were banished to the Netherworld.

"He didn't take being banished lightly. Asmodeus was a proud archangel, and the strongest amongst us. I saw the hatred in his eyes when he departed. I knew then, it wouldn't be the last we'd see of him. I just never imagined it could be like this."

Gabriel slammed his fist on the great table. Kara and the others jumped. "He will pay dearly for what he has done!"

Camael shook her head. "I cannot understand how he could consume all those archangels' souls — and still live. His body shouldn't be able to withstand it. We creatures were not created to endure so much power. He must have learned something that we are ignorant of. It makes no sense to me."

Michael turned to Gabriel. "Get the troops ready. We leave in fifteen minutes. We must act now, while there are still some of us left who can." He sheathed the blazing blade in a leather sheath wrapped tightly around his ankle. Kara couldn't see the flames anymore. He straightened and shared a look with Gabriel. "We know where he'll be. It's time."

Gabriel nodded in silent agreement. He turned and addressed the others. "Guardians, follow me. We're going to meet with the rest of the troops in the atrium — no, not you Kara."

"What!" Kara's voice rose before she could control it. "I'm a guardian. I'm coming too."

"No, you will stay with Raphael — "

"I'm not staying behind!" Kara's temper flared. She saw the irritation in Gabriel's face, but she couldn't control herself. She had risked her life to get here and fight alongside her friends.

This was her fight, too; they couldn't take that away from her. "I'm going."

"No."

"Why not? This is crazy!"

"Because we know Asmodeus intends to kill you. You're safe here."

Kara clasped her shaking hands into fists. "He intends to kill everyone! I'm not going to stay here and hide like a coward."

"We need you safe, Kara —"

"I'm going! He used me to kill all those mortals, and now angels. And you expect me to sit tight? You don't know me. I'm not staying behind."

Michael pushed past Gabriel. His eyes fixed on Kara. "Can you imagine what would happen if he killed you and ingested *your* power? Camael tells us that he is absorbing the essence of archangels. What if he is planning on embracing yours? What would happen if he succeeded? Can you think of the devastation he could cause with elemental power surging through him? He would become a creature that no one would be able to vanquish. Not even an inferno blade could harm him. We would all perish."

Kara could only stare. She hadn't thought of that. Although it hurt to hear it, she knew Michael was right. She would have to stay behind. Kara pressed her lips into a hard line. She caught David staring at her. He gave her a weak smile. Kara stared at the floor.

Satisfied, Michael walked past her without another word and vanished behind the chamber's door.

Gabriel stood by the doorway. "Danielle. David. You're coming with us. It's time we paid a little visit to my long lost *brother*."

Kara's mother went to her and embraced her. "Don't do anything stupid," her mother whispered in her ear. "I know you, Kara. Be careful. I'll see you soon. Promise."

Kara hugged her mother tightly for a moment, and then let her go. She forced a smile.

David tried to catch Kara's attention, but she didn't look at him. She was angry and ashamed. It wasn't fair.

With tightness in her chest, Kara watched them disappear behind the door.

CHAPTER 16
DOWN UNDER

Kara paced around the chamber for what felt like an hour. Raphael repeatedly tried to get her to sit, but Kara was restless. Every time she sat down, she would jump back up, with images of her mother and David being torn apart by demons overwhelming her mind. She thought she was going mad.

Kara shuddered at the image of a grey and solemn Horizon, with nothing but dark ashes rolling away in gusts of wind. No. She would never let that happen.

"Kara, please sit down," pleaded Raphael, as she fidgeted at Camael's side. "You're making me anxious. It won't do any good to fuss about. You need to calm yourself."

"I can't," grumbled Kara. "This is all my fault. And I'm stuck here, helpless. How would you feel, if you were me? It's not fair!" Kara kicked a chair. She realized how childish this was to the archangels, but she didn't care. It felt good to vent.

Raphael pressed her hands on her hips. "Well, it's *not* your fault. You have to stop blaming yourself —"

"It *is* my fault. Without me, none of this would have happened. Asmodeus wouldn't have been able to use the Mirror of Souls to strike the mortal world, and use it as a diversion to attack Horizon. Don't you see? This is my fault!"

"You are not responsible for a madman's plan. He is doing this, not you. It is his desire to dominate all things—that's the cause for all of this madness. You were not abetting him, Kara. You tried to stop him—"

"Exactly. I tried and failed." Kara slumped into a chair. She thought suddenly of Jenny and Peter. "Raphael, do you know if my friends Peter and Jenny made it back safely?" Kara glanced at the archangel anxiously.

Raphael, who had gone across the room to fetch a vial of purple liquid for Camael, returned and sat down next to Kara. "I know that they were still on their mission when all this mess happened. They're probably on the eighth plane with the rest of the stranded guardians. They're safe Kara, I'm sure of it."

Kara nodded. Part of her relaxed with the assurance that her friends were safe—at least they would be spared, if things went terribly wrong. She wondered if Michael's special blade would be strong enough. Her powers might have been of some use to them. She could have found a way to help them, and not get caught by Asmodeus; she was sure of it. She should be there with them, fighting. Anything was better than sitting here useless, with the invalids. This was hopeless. Kara tightened her grip on the chair's arm-rest. Her fingers dug into the soft wood. Her mother and David were out there—probably getting killed — while she sat and played house with the giant healer. It was wrong. It felt wrong. She had to do something.

BOOM!

The chamber door flew open. An oracle stood on his crystal ball behind the doorway. His wispy white hair stood on end on the top of his head, as though an electric current ran through his body. With crazed blue eyes he searched the room. He danced nervously atop his ball, his silver robe rippling around him. Finally, he found Kara.

"Ah! There she is! Quickly, quickly, Miss Clara!" He waved his arms in the air theatrically, and Kara was certain he would slip and fall off his crystal at any moment. "We must make haste, we must make haste!"

Kara jumped to her feet and ran up to the oracle. "What is it, oracle? What's happened? Is my mother all right? Is it David?" Dread filled her mind. The image of a higher demon's gaping jaw tearing out David's soul haunted her. Coldness swept through her.

The oracle tugged at his beard nervously. "Terrible things, terrible things, Miss Clara. We must go now. Quickly. There is no time to waste."

"But where are we going, oracle?" But somehow Kara already knew where.

"To the High Council. We must hurry. They need you." The oracle was hysterical. He kept glancing over his shoulder as if expecting someone were following him.

Determined, Kara stepped forward, but Raphael pulled her back.

"No, Kara," said Raphael, her face set. "You heard what Michael said. If Asmodeus means to kill you … and he exploits your powers, all is lost. I cannot allow you to go. You must stay here with us."

"No!" The oracle grabbed Raphael's front robe hastily. "She is meant to be there. I have seen it! It is how it's supposed to be. She is the one. She will save us from this evil. If Miss Clara is not permitted to go …" the oracle let go of Raphael's robe and stared above their heads to nothing in particular. "Then all shall be lost."

A shiver passed through Kara. What was the oracle saying? Kara was at a loss. She knew oracles could see into the future — and this one had seen her at the High Council. It was a sign. She had to go.

"I'm going with him." Kara stared into Raphael's beautiful face. "You heard him. I'm supposed to be there. It's important, Raphael. They need me." She prayed the oracle's foresight was enough to convince the archangel.

Raphael's worried expression made Kara more nervous. She could see the woman struggling with something internally. At last she spoke. "If it is as the oracle has seen it, then it shall be. I cannot change what is foretold by the oracles. Go, Kara. And may the souls protect you."

Kara jumped into the woman's large arms and hugged her as best she could, even though her arms couldn't wrap themselves around Raphael's extra large shoulders. She kissed her on the cheek. "Thank you."

Without another second to waste, Kara followed the oracle out the door.

Kara ran alongside the crystal ball up a dirt path leading away from the mountain and down to a lush valley of green and yellow hills. The loud crushing of rock coming from under the crystal ball silenced the sound of her boots hitting the ground. She struggled to keep up with the oracle. He was surprisingly fast. His enormous crystal rolled up the hills effortlessly, without slowing down. Soon they had crossed the valley and found themselves in a dense forest.

A flicker of movement appeared in the corner of Kara's eye.

A large creature charged from the trees. Before she had time to react, it slashed at her face. Pain exploded from her head, and she was knocked to the ground. She rolled over and looked at her attacker. It stood on two muscular hind legs with hoofed feet. It had long arms and hands thick with razor-sharp yellow claws. Its skin was wet and raw, as though only flesh covered the bones without the skin. Black liquid spilled from a large gaping maw in the center of its bulky chest. Much to Kara's horror, it had no head.

The demon leaped into the air. Kara sprung to her feet as the creature landed inches before her. The scent of decay reached her nose. Its large claws lashed out at her. Kara jumped back. With her soul blade clutched in her hand, she struck out at the creature—and missed. The demon eluded her attack easily. With its powerful legs it moved unnaturally fast. It came at her again, its mouth stretched wide. Kara could see hundreds of pointy yellow teeth with flesh wedged in between some of them. She sidestepped and thrust her blade into the creature's abdomen. She yanked her arm across in an arc. The cut was deep. The creature wailed in anger. It fell to its knees, cradling its wound. She walked towards the creature, her blade at her side, ready to finish it off—

Suddenly, the oracle's giant crystal ploughed over the demon. Kara heard a muffled cry and then only the crushing sound of bones turning to dust. Kara stared at a flattened mess of flesh and bones. There was no way to determine what part of the creature she was looking at. She glanced at the oracle in surprise. His face was set in a hard line.

"Dirty little beasts. All of them, dirty, filthy beasts! Think they can come here and destroy our home! I don't think so!"

"Wow ... you really showed him, didn't you," laughed Kara. She looked over the ball to see if it were stained with some of the demon's remains. It wasn't. It was perfectly clean, as if it had never crushed through flesh.

Kara heard a twig snap. She whirled around. Ten more headless demons came thrashing through the forest. Their angry limbs flailed as they scampered towards them. Kara froze. She tried to call forth her elemental power, but there was nothing but a dull ache inside her chest.

There was a sudden pop, and a tiny round door swung open from the crystal ball.

The oracle jumped down and pointed hastily towards the door. "In you go! Quickly, Miss Clara! We don't have much time. The beasts are coming."

Kara gawked openmouthed at the perfectly cut round hole on the giant crystal. The edges were smooth, as though someone had cut it with a laser. She had never noticed a door before. But now it stood ajar like a well-hidden secret.

"You want me to go in there?" Kara picked at the edges with her blade.

The oracle looked nervously down the path towards the oncoming horde of demons. "There's no time to argue, Miss Clara! There are too many of the nasty beasts!"

"How am I supposed to get though? The door's way too small and I'm way too big to fit in there —" She poked her head in the glass compartment. It looked exactly like the inside of a large bowl. The sun's rays shone through the smooth surface and reflected a myriad of colors along its curved walls. Brilliant little rainbows blinked into Kara's eyes. It was beautiful inside and she wondered if the oracles slept in there.

She felt a sudden pressure on her back and flew into the crystal ball's belly. She landed head first, her legs followed and twisted clumsily behind her. Once her feet were in she managed to get herself into a sitting position. It was tight, can of sardines tight, but Kara fit nonetheless. What choice did she have? She could see shadows of trees around her. It was like looking through a thick bottle. The shapes were distorted, but she could still make them out.

"Hang on, Clara. It could get a little bumpy."

"Yeah, thanks for the heads up," yelled Kara from inside the crystal's stomach, a little annoyed, and suddenly feeling a little claustrophobic.

The door shut with a bang, and the edges disappeared. Kara couldn't make it out anymore. It was as though the door had never existed. The oracle hoisted himself back up atop his crystal and swung his beard over his shoulder. The sounds of grunts reached her and she saw silhouettes of the demons approaching. They were almost upon them.

Suddenly, Kara was thrown against the wall with unimaginable force. Pinned to one of the sides of the crystal, she looked around. Shapes passed her by in a blur. She couldn't tell what was up and what was down. It was like a maelstrom of images thrown together. She felt herself spinning endlessly. It reminded her of one of the rides from the town fair, the one that used to make her throw up. She was glad she couldn't, it was too tight a space.

And when Kara thought the spinning would never end, the crystal stopped suddenly. She fell flat on her face, her legs bent awkwardly behind her. With a pop, the door flew open and Kara saw the oracle's face peer inside.

"I apologize for the bumpy ride, Miss Clara. But it was necessary." The oracle looked behind him. "It'll take a good long time before they catch up, those filthy creatures." He beamed at her.

"It's okay … really." Kara climbed out of the confining space. She fell to the ground and rubbed her head. "Just glad to be out."

She looked around and realized they were out of the forest. A large brass elevator stood before them; the metal gleamed in the sunlight. Kara blinked the light from her eyes. The doors were open, and Kara couldn't see an operator. It was empty, save for a small wooden stool propped against the side wall.

"Where's the operator?" Kara searched the grounds around the elevator. There were no primates of any sort. It seemed the elevator had been abandoned.

The oracle clambered up his crystal and rolled over for a closer inspection. "I don't know. There's no one there, that's for sure." He straightened himself. "No matter, it'll work just the same."

Kara remembered the flesh wedged in the demon's teeth. She had the nasty feeling that one of the headless demons had eaten the elevator operator. She prayed she was wrong, and that it had run away and was hiding in the woods. She wouldn't blame the poor creature if it were hiding. Their world had gone mad. Their torn bodies were scattered around the desert floor. She shuddered and pushed the thoughts out of her head. They needed to get to level six.

Kara stepped into the elevator and turned around. She frowned. "Are you coming?"

The oracle shook his head sadly. "No, Miss. I must remain here. This is your journey, not mine. You must go alone."

Kara had hoped for the oracle's company on the way to the council. She didn't know what to expect. An extra person would have been appreciated. "So what am I supposed to do when I get to the council? What did you see, oracle?" Kara tried to hide the regret in her voice, but it sounded more like fear.

The little man interlaced his long beard between his fingers. "I cannot tell you, for fear that it might change the outcome of the events. I cannot change what is to be, just as you cannot change your fate. I can only tell you that you must go to level six. The rest is up to you, my dear."

Kara cringed. She wanted more information from the oracle. She hated riddles.

"Well, thanks anyway, oracle. Wish me luck. And I hope there was a happy ending in those visions of yours."

The oracle smiled and waved his little hand. "Good luck, Clara. May the souls protect you."

"It's *Kara*—not *Clara*," laughed Kara at the look of surprise on the oracle's face. She turned to the control panel and pressed the button for the sixth floor. There was a *ding*, and the doors slid shut.

After about a minute, there was another *ding*, followed by a jolt, and the doors opened to reveal a dark grey sky. Powerful winds rolled into the small compartment, and Kara felt the elevator shake as though a giant was tossing it to and fro like a ball. She held onto the sides and struggled to the doorway.

The dark skies were heavy with black clouds and the crack of thunder. There was no trace of the beautiful white clouds and the piercing blue sky of level six. It looked sick, plagued by the Netherworld.

Kara clutched the sides as another gust of wind shook the elevator. She squinted. Were there any sky-cars left or had they all been destroyed, too? She couldn't hear the tap-tap-tap of their motors over the roar of thunder. Maybe they were there, hiding in the clouds.

"Sam! Sam!" cried Kara into the wind. "Sam, I need your help! Sam — are you there?"

Desperation filled her as she waited for the little bird. If he didn't come, how would she get across? She couldn't fly. Even the prison guards were busy fighting off demons at Operations. She couldn't hope to catch a ride with them now. How did the others get across? Maybe they used the last of the sky-cars. Kara searched the dark skies for any sign of movement. Her hair blew into her face. Nothing moved but the wind. How was she going to get across?

A faint tap made its way to her ears. She heard it again, only closer this time.

Kara gazed into the blackened skies in search of the sound. A tiny white spot pierced through a grey cloud. She recognized the sky-car's white body. The car dove towards her, and in a flash it hovered at the door. A large white bird with black wings stood at the front of his flying device. He wore a red cap with the numbers 2555 stitched across it in gold. The corners of his yellow beak were pulled back into a smile.

"Sam, at your service, Miss Kara!" cried the bird. He flapped his wings and hopped onto the metal T gear. He tipped his hat and bowed overdramatically. "Like my new ride? The prison guards destroyed my other one. I had to use all my tips to purchase this new baby." He puffed out his chest and beamed.

Without a moment's hesitation, Kara jumped into the sky-car. It swayed to the side with her weight, and she clung to the seats. It looked exactly like the other sky-car. "It's beautiful, Sam. Look, I'm so glad you're here. I need to get to the Council of Ministers right away. How fast can this thing go?" She fastened her seatbelt. She had ridden in the flying cars before and recalled the bumpy ride.

Sam spread his wings. "Faster than lightning! Here we go. Hang on!" Sam pushed all his weight forward onto the gear. The sky-car kicked into life and sped away.

Kara was pinned to her seat as the flying car gained speed. Shapes passed her in a blur. She could see the floating buildings approaching fast. Before she knew it, the sky-car slowed to a stop and hovered above a large landing zone. Kara unclasped her seat belt and jumped down. She stood on a metal platform on the highest part of the council building.

"Oh, dear." Sam took off his cap and placed it on his breast. His eyes were wet.

Kara looked around. Weapons lay broken in piles of metal. Piles of uniforms and robes were scattered on the ground. A chill rolled up her back. There had been a bloodbath here. She thought of her mother and David. A cry escaped her lips. Were any of these clothes theirs?

Without thanking Sam, or giving him payment, Kara ran madly down across the platform and pulled open the metal door at the far end. Hot stale air brushed her nostrils, and a faint smell of rot. She raced down the hallway. More piles of clothes lay crumpled on the ground. Her throat tightened and another whimper escaped her lips. She held onto the soul blade her mother had given her, suppressing the trembling in her fingers.

Soon Kara reached the massive brass doors leading to the council chamber. She noticed one of the doors wasn't closed entirely. There was enough space for her to sneak in. She could hear a loud commotion as she neared. Her nervousness increased. She heard a scream. It sounded like her mother's voice.

Kara squeezed herself through the doors.

At first she saw Asmodeus standing up on the dais at the opposite end of the round chamber. His hands were clutched around something in his chest. He was laughing. Michael stood a few paces before him. An expression of shock plastered over his face.

The glass dome was shattered and shards of glass littered the floor like a giant crystal carpet. A gust of wind blew dust into Kara's face. The only source of light came from the few metal lanterns that lined the round chamber. She crept closer. Angels lay in broken piles, their bodies twisted unnaturally. Their insides spilled out from many wounds, as demons feasted on their life lights. Cries of anguish reached her ears. Cold rattled inside her. It was the massacre she had feared. She searched for her mother and David, but there were no signs of them anywhere.

Laughter rose above the whistling winds and the cries of angels. Kara watched as the demon lord pulled out a blade made of fire from his chest, laughing. It was the inferno. He stood unscathed, without any sign of injury or pain. The demon lord twirled the inferno dagger in his fingers with a look of triumph on his face.

There was a sudden flash.

A mixture of fire and black lightning surged into the air. Kara heard a cry. Michael collapsed to the ground, the inferno blade protruding from his chest. Instantly, he was ablaze in a golden fire. Kara heard a crackling sound, and then the fire went out. With a soft clang the blade hit the floor. A cloud of brilliant particles hovered above where the body had lain. They glimmered in the soft light and disappeared in a gust of wind.

Michael, the Legion's commander, was no more.

Chapter 17
Making a Choice

Silence. Kara felt numb, her body stiff. The benches swarmed with lesser demons. Hundreds of demons crawled along the walls; their wet twisted bodies gleamed in the soft light. Cracks and thumps resonated in the chamber as the beasts fought each other for a better seat. The air reeked of rotten flesh and blood.

A large angel sat on the ground opposite her. White lesions covered his dark skin. Beams of light spilled from his many wounds, but Kara could see that he was alert as he clung to a nearby bench. Gabriel's eyes caught hers. It pained her to see the strain on his face. For a moment, she thought he was trying to communicate something to her. His face was twisted in a deep scowl. He seemed upset to see her there. She realized he was terrified that she had disobeyed him. She shook her head, pleading with her eyes and tried to mouth that it was okay. His disappointing frown made her stop. Kara wasn't exactly sure what she was supposed to do either way. The oracle had said she was meant to be here — only he hadn't filled in the rest.

Asmodeus clapped his hands. His black hair glimmered in the gentle light. "Bravo, bravo. What a performance. I kill myself—I'm so talented. But alas, what a waste of a powerful soul. It could have given me more power."

He raised his arms before him. He wore his usual blood red suit tailored to perfection over his large body. He looked at Kara. "There you are my daughter. Once again you arrive just in the nick of time for the show." Asmodeus snapped his fingers.

Two higher demons seized her. She tried to break free, but the higher demons' grips were too strong. "Take your hands off me! Let go of me!"

With his hands clasped behind his back, Asmodeus strolled around the dais. "Do you like to play games, Kara? We never did play any games together, you and I. As your father, don't you think we should have played some games?"

"Go to hell."

"My, my … that's not how to speak to your father, dear daughter. I might have to wash out that mouth of yours." The demon lord frowned.

Kara wished she could spit in his face. "You're not my father," she hissed.

"Oh, but I am. You see—I created you; therefore I am your father. And as your father, I get to decide what to do with you. And now I wish to play a game. Zadkiel —bring them."

Kara heard a commotion at the far end of the chamber behind the dais. The traitorous Zadkiel appeared from the shadows. His bald head gleamed in the light. He made his way through a wall of demons that hissed and spat as he went. Two shapes struggled in his grasp. Coldness filled Kara's breast. David and her mother were in the archangel's clutches. Kara watched as he dragged them to the center of the chamber by their necks. Kara let out a whimper at the sight of her mother's face. Deep gashes covered her cheeks and forehead, and one of her legs was bent awkwardly. She struggled to keep up. David seemed to be in better shape. Their eyes met. She saw him shake his head. Kara felt a jolt of electricity pass through her body. This could not be happening.

"Let them go you monster! I'll kill you … I swear I'll kill you if you hurt them." Kara's anger flared inside her. The elemental power awakened instantly, as if she had turned on a switch. The power poured through her, faster than ever before. She felt the warmness of it surge through every fiber of her body. It encased her in a protective shell of strength. She trembled in rage.

Asmodeus raised an eyebrow. "Monster? You disappoint me, daughter. I thought you of all people would understand why I have done this. That hunger for power that flows inside you right now, is the same as mine … more or less. We are alike, you and I—"

"I am nothing like you," spat Kara. "I don't kill innocent people. I am not a monster like you." She glared at the demon lord. She knew she was on the threshold of releasing her power. She knew she would not be able to control it. And yet she willed it forth.

"Innocent. Nobody is *innocent* anymore." Asmodeus adjusted his red bowtie and smoothed the front of his jacket. "Take your *amour* for instance. He is not as innocent as you might think, my dear. Mingling with mortal women — breaking the forbidden laws. Perhaps we should teach him a lesson — "

A surge of electric current shot from Asmodeus's hand. It struck David. He screamed and fell to his knees. He shook violently and tiny black sparks snaked in and around his body.

At that same instant, Kara released her power. Her body thrust out rays of gold. She heard a muffled scream, and felt the blasts of an explosion on either side of her. With tremendous force, she directed a beam of energy towards the dais. It hit Asmodeus. His body disappeared under a cocoon of golden vines. Kara heard a sizzling sound. The golden tendrils snapped and fell to the ground like a tangle of rope.

Asmodeus stood untouched.

He clapped his hands again, clearly amused. "Bravo, daughter. I must applaud your courage." He raised his arms dramatically. "But as you can see ... your power cannot harm me, dearest. I am too powerful now ... thanks to the souls of my fellow archangels. I'm just very *annoyed* that you destroyed my favorite suit." He brushed the front of his jacket.

Kara felt her power diminish like the dying flame that hangs on the point of the wick. The oracle had told her to come to the council. He had said that she was meant to be there — to do something important. She was convinced it was to use her powers against the demon lord. But it hadn't worked. What was she to do now? Clearly, the demon lord was much more powerful than anyone—even her elemental powers had no effect on him. Fear crept into the back of her mind. What was she to do? What had she done?

She felt strong hands grab her again.

"Can't get rid of us that easily, monkey lover," spat the higher demon. He smiled coolly at her and tightened his grip. "Soon, you will all be dead."

"I'd rather love a monkey than a filthy devil any day." Kara said, struggling in his grasp. "Let go of me, you freak!" She kicked him hard with her legs, but the demon wouldn't let go. He simply laughed at her, clearly enjoying himself. Another higher demon took hold of her other arm. Their identical faces grinned at her. She saw hunger flash in their black eyes. She wanted to gouge them out.

"Well, now that's settled. Moving on to better things … ah, Danielle." Asmodeus looked over to her mother. His face softened and he put his hands dramatically over his chest. "Still as beautiful as I remembered...hmm—no, more beautiful than I remembered. Perhaps later we could rekindle what we once had? What do you say, my darling wife?"

Danielle lifted her eyes painfully. "How could you do this, Samuel? How could you do this to our daughter!"

An evil smile spread over the demon lord's face. He straightened and smoothed down his hair. "Zadkiel—leave the boy and bring her to me. I want to look into my wife's beautiful eyes."

Kara watched as the archangel dragged her mother across the floor and up to the dais. Zadkiel threw her on the ground. Kara cried out and fought feverously against the higher demons. But they wouldn't let go. A sickening laugh escaped from Asmodeus—he was enjoying causing her mother pain. She raised her head and watched the scene through her bangs. He reached down and lifted her mother by the neck. Her feet dangled beneath her like a puppet's pulled up on its strings. He raised his other hand and snapped his fingers. Black energy snaked around them.

"Now, dearest daughter. You must choose." Asmodeus pointed to David. "The young man you love so *desperately*...or your beloved mother?"

Coldness washed over Kara.

David stood in the center of the chamber alone. He turned and looked at Kara. He smiled reassuringly, but Kara could see the fear in his eyes. His fingers twitched nervously.

Asmodeus enjoyed seeing the distress in his daughter's eyes. He smiled and spoke in a nonchalant manner. "Who will live ... and who will die. You must choose." He laughed softly to himself. "I would be a great game show host, don't you think? I certainly have the charisma."

Kara met David's eyes. She could see him struggling to hide his fear. She ached at his pain. "Please … please, father, I'll do anything. Don't hurt them. I'll do whatever you ask of me."

"This is what I ask of you. You must choose … and choose wisely."

Kara looked from her mother to David. She trembled uncontrollably. "I can't … I can't choose between them …"

"You must. If you don't … I will kill them both."

Kara redoubled her attempts to get away from the higher demons, kicking out her legs like a crazed beast. The higher demons retaliated by stabbing her with their death blades. She cried out, as the poison burned her. If only she could get away.

"It's okay, Kara. Don't worry about me," said David, his voice cracking. "Save your mother. But promise me one thing … promise me that you're going to kick this fool's butt." He stretched his trembling lips into a thin smile. She knew he was trying to be brave. David McGowan couldn't show fear.

Kara let out a cry and her body went limp. How was she to choose between the boy she loved and her mother? How could anyone choose? Kara couldn't choose. She stopped struggling against the demons.

"I … cannot," she said finally, the words burning on her lips. "How can I?"

"*Choose!*" roared Asmodeus. Debris fell from above and showered Kara in a blanket of dust. "Or they both die! You stupid girl!"

Her mother screamed. Blank tendrils wrapped themselves around her body. The black vapors were squeezing the life out of her. Kara knew she was at death's door.

Kara's lips trembled. She looked at David. He stared at the ground, unwilling to meet her eyes. She wanted desperately to reach out to him. *David*, she called inside her mind. *What do I do?*

Asmodeus chuckled. "I'm so disappointed with you, my daughter. I thought for sure you would have chosen the boy over your mother. Well … I guess I'll have to make the decision for you."

Black lighting shot out of the demon lord's hand.

It struck David in the chest.

He wailed as the current worked around him, burning his angel body. He crumbled to the ground. His body shook and the black tendrils enveloped him. The sound of flesh blistering and scorching made her feel sick. Black vapors emanated from his body. They ate through his skin like an acid. A terrible scream escaped Kara. She couldn't stop screaming.

"Let her go." Kara heard Asmodeus say suddenly.

She fell to her knees. She realized her arms were free. Kara struggled to her feet and ran over to David. His angel skin had disappeared and had been replaced by a shell of brilliant light.

Kara cradled his body carefully against her chest. "David! David!"

David opened his eyes slowly. "Kara?"

"Yes, I'm here. You're going to be fine." She gently caressed his face.

"Kara. I'm sorry." His voice cracked, and Kara could hardly hear him anymore. She leaned forward closer and angled her ear to his lips.

"There's nothing to be sorry about. This is my fault. All of it is my fault."

With the last of his energy, David squeezed Kara's hand. "I wish … I wish that we could have met as mortals. We could have had a life together—you and me. You are my soul mate, Kara Nightingale. Our souls were meant to be together. And now I'm going to die, without ever really having the chance to be with you."

Kara pulled David closer to her. "No … you're going to be okay. I—I'm going to get you to Raphael. She's going to make you better, I promise."

"Kill him, Kara…"

"David!"

Hot white light shone through David's body. His solid form burst into a million brilliant little particles. They hovered for a moment above David's pile of clothes, like a cloud of stars. They flickered and then began to rise, caught in the invisible wind.

Kara let out a cry. She jumped up and flailed her arms desperately in the air, trying to catch David's essence. But the glowing particles passed through her fingers and vanished from her hands like melted snow flakes.

With a last struggle, Kara dropped her hands to her side and stared up into the dark grey sky where David had disappeared.

CHAPTER 18
LAST CALL

Kara stood alone in the center of the chamber, a constant ringing hammered in her ears. Her spirit was broken. David was gone forever. He was dead. Asmodeus had killed him. The floor began to waver. She closed her eyes, and let herself fall.

She heard a whisper of her name—it felt so far away. She lay on the cold stone floor, numb to the world around her. She felt hands gently pick her up and arms around her. Kara opened her eyes.

"Mom."

Kara sobbed into her mother's chest. She cried out David's name. But as a guardian angel, no tears came. No release from the pain like when she'd been a mortal and her tears could wash away her sadness. In Horizon she had no release, and so the pain was a hundred times worse.

"What a beautiful family reunion, don't you think?" Kara heard Asmodeus say. "Finally, we are a family once again. Ah … I feel all tingly inside."

Kara lifted her head from her mother's shoulder. "You … are not my family," she hissed, and added as much venom to her words as she could.

Asmodeus lifted his hands in defeat. "Now, now, dear daughter. Don't be angry with me, although I hear that teenagers are *not* supposed to get along with their parents. So I believe your hatred towards me is completely natural. He was no good for you, Kara, I promise. I can give you as many boy toys as you want. Just say the word, and they're yours."

Asmodeus stepped off the platform gracefully and sauntered towards them.

"You're sick."

"Not at all. I feel great." The demon lord kicked out his feet and danced about the room. "I've never been better! I am undefeated, you see. I have all the power now. I will crush what's left of the mortal world and rule the spirit world. Horizon is mine at last." His face cracked into an evil grin. He looked up and addressed the hoards of demons that lurked in and around the chamber seats. "Demons! As promised, Horizon is ours. And today we shall feast — feast on the souls of angels!"

The entire chamber went up in a roar. Higher and lesser demons alike joined in what Kara thought sounded like some type of ceremonial chant. They threw back their heads and howled. The room shook, and Kara felt the floor beneath her vibrate. Demons jumped from the walls and landed amidst the mob of creatures below. Their chanting grew louder. They circled around Kara and her mother. The smell of rot was mixed with the sour stink of demon breath. Kara saw the terror in her mother's eyes. She felt it too. They were about to become a main course on the demon's menu.

"What's going to happen to my mom and me?" asked Kara, with panic in her voice.

Asmodeus sighed. "You've made it very clear to me that you don't want to be part of my ... family. So what do you think will happen to you? You're a clever girl. I'll give you a hint—it rhymes with breath—"

The demon lord laughed and twirled on the spot.

The clouds parted suddenly, and a ray of sunshine seeped through from above. It lit a tiny part of the chamber in a soft yellow light for a moment, and then went out. But a flicker of light had caught Kara's attention—the inferno blade lay a few feet from her.

The demon lord pulled at his cuffs. "I'm definitely going to need a new suit. But not before we do a little cleansing first." He looked up and his eyes landed on Gabriel. He smiled. "Zadkiel. I need you to bring me that pathetic archangel over there. I'm in need of a little tonic to brighten my mood."

Kara looked over to Gabriel. He hadn't moved from his spot, as he clung to a nearby bench for support. With his jaw set, the big archangel looked determined to die without fear—to die the true death.

And then it hit her. She knew what she was supposed to do.

Kara pushed away from her mother gently and rushed over to the dagger. She picked it up. The flames spilled around her hand and arm, but she felt only a slight tingling sensation. She gripped it firmly in her hand. It felt light and natural.

Asmodeus's face twisted. He laughed out loud. "What's this? Wait a minute, Zadkiel ... my daughter wishes to do me more harm, don't you, Kara."

Kara ignored him. Instead, she walked calmly over to where her father stood, looking elegant even in his ruin red suit. The blade hung by her side.

"That blade cannot hurt me, silly girl. Don't you get it? I am eternal. Nothing can harm me, ever again."

Kara stood before the demon lord. She sensed the dagger's power in her right hand. The golden flames tickled her skin. She thought of David. She remembered his beautiful blue eyes—her best friend—her mentor. She remembered his soft lips on hers when they had kissed the first time—she had been in love with him since then. She remembered how amazing it had felt to be held in his strong arms—his face had evaporated into nothingness in front of her. She would never see him again.

Asmodeus giggled like a schoolboy. "This day is proving to be better than I'd anticipated. My daughter ... trying to kill me ... once again." The demon lord clapped his hands excitedly.

With no expression on her face, Kara locked her eyes with her father's.

"You're wrong. This blade is not for you, dear father. It's for me — "

Kara drove the dagger into her chest. She heard her mother scream.

She focused on Asmodeus. Her elemental power, the dagger's power, and her angel essence combined. She felt the three sources combine into one unimaginable power. She ignored the excruciating pain and focused only on Asmodeus. He needed to die.

She felt a burning sensation, then the smell of burnt flesh. She looked down at her body. Her angel skin was slipping off her, into a puddle on the floor. She was melting away like a wax figure. Soon, her entire skin was gone. Only a shell of bright golden light remained. Kara knew she was dying, like David. She knew she didn't have much time before her body dissolved completely.

She focused all her energy on Asmodeus. She raised her arms in the air. Golden light blasted through her hands and hit her demon father.

He staggered backwards, surprised.

"What's this?" His body was consumed in a golden fire. He waved his hands frantically. Kara heard the crackling of fire. Asmodeus screamed and ran blindly around the chamber, desperately trying to put out the flames. His loud screeching echoed throughout the chamber, and then he was still. Only the flames moved as they danced in and around his body. Kara could see to the other side of the chamber through large gaps in his body. He tipped over and hit the floor. His flaming body exploded into a puff of black dust. Small particles hung in the air for a moment and then disappeared into nothing.

Kara felt her life force leaving her body. She managed to walk over to the spot where David had died and collapsed to the ground.

She can hear her mother's soft voice calling out to her. But she cannot see her. She tries to answer, but her mouth will not move. The sweet sound of her mother's voice wraps around her. Kara is glad her mother is finally safe. The Legion is safe. Horizon is safe. She has done her duty.

She knows that she is ready, and she lets herself go.

CHAPTER 19
A PENTHOUSE IN THE STARS

A soft breeze smells of pine trees and earth. The soft murmur of people talking flows around like leaves caught in breeze. Bottles clank together, and the clatter of metal hitting metal reverberates. Something heavy scrapes the floor, dripping liquid splashes, and then a loud thud, as though a door had been closed.

Kara opened her eyes. Blurred shapes moved around her. She blinked. After a moment, her eyesight returned. She looked around. Red light spilled from a window above, casting a warm glow around the round room. Kara recognized the room immediately. She was in Raphael's healing chamber. With some effort, Kara sat up and inspected herself. She was dressed in a pair of comfortable white linen pajamas, like the kind from an expensive hotel. Why was she here and wearing pajamas? Suddenly the memories came flooding in.

David. Asmodeus. The inferno blade.

She peeled away at some buttons and examined her chest. No signs of any puncture wounds. It had never happened—it had all been a terrible dream. A red haired woman was sitting calmly in a chair nearby, Camael, the archangel who had been hurt by Asmodeus. Raphael was still tending to Camael's wounds. It wasn't a dream.

David really was dead.

"Kara!" Raphael rushed over. She took Kara's hand in hers and squeezed it affectionately. "I was so worried. I—I wasn't sure I could heal you—but I did!" She looked at Kara's puzzled face. "You had just enough life force in you for me to bring you back. I can't explain it—maybe it has something to do with your *elemental* part, but I'm just glad it worked."

Kara looked into her blazing green eyes. She tried to smile, but her face was numb. She couldn't even bring herself to thank the woman. She didn't feel so excited to be back. Not without David. She sensed Raphael reading her thoughts. Abashed, Kara lowered her eyes and stared at her hands.

"Listen to me, Kara." Raphael brushed a lock of hair behind Kara's ear. Her eyes were kind. "I loved David, too, and I miss him terribly. But we can't change what happened." She cupped Kara's face into her large hands. "Kara. You saved us. You saved the Legion. We would all be gone if it hadn't been for your courage and quick thinking. I know if David were here now, he would be so proud of you. I am proud of you. We all are. So is your mother."

"M—my mother. She's okay, right?" She vaguely remembered her mother's voice calling out to her before she passed out. Kara prayed that nothing had happened to her.

"Yes," said Raphael, "your mother is fine. She and Gabriel brought you to me."

The image of Gabriel's body covered in wounds rose in Kara's mind. "So ... what happened after I blacked out? Where are the demons now?"

"Gone. After they saw their master killed, they ran away like scared little rats. They crawled back to the Netherworld — where they belong."

"What about Zadkiel?"

The archangel let out a loud sigh. "Unfortunately, the traitorous Zadkiel escaped. Gabriel said that Zadkiel ran as soon as he saw his master die, just like a true coward. Who knows into what hole he's crawled." Kara could think of one.

"So, Horizon is slowly picking up the pieces and mending itself," continued Raphael. "We still have lots to do, but eventually we'll get there. Horizon will be just as beautiful as before. And soon all the GAs will be back at work saving mortals. You'll be back at your old job before you know it."

Kara couldn't speak. The words wouldn't come out. They burned at the back of her throat. She just shook her head that she understood.

The archangel shrugged. "Let's get you changed. The Chief is expecting you, Kara. He's very excited about you visiting him." At that, Kara lifted her eyes.

"Yes," continued the archangel. "He wants to have a chat with you. I'm guessing that he wants a full account of what happened. He's very thorough … make sure you tell him everything. Don't leave anything out." Kara nodded that she wouldn't.

Kara stared at her recently polished boots — they were so shiny they looked wet. The elevator's gentle sway made her move slightly from left to right. The elevator's operator, an excessively large toothed baboon by the name of 3B52, had survived the attacks — he couldn't shut up about it. He tried relentlessly to get her to talk, but she only heard muffles and stared at the floor.

Ding. The elevator doors slid open. Kara peered out. White light blinded her vision. It was like stepping into the sun. She heard a clang behind her, and she knew the elevator had departed. Kara walked further into the light, and when it dispersed she was in a giant penthouse sort of apartment.

The room was elegantly furnished with plush carpets and soft looking sofas and armchairs. Twenty-foot high windows ran the length of the room on all four sides. A black sky glinting with crystals shone behind the glass, and Kara thought they looked strangely like stars. She felt heat on the side of her head. She turned around and covered her eyes. Incredibly, Kara was staring at the sun. She ran towards the closest window. She pressed her forehead against the glass and peered out into outer space.

The large apartment floated in a galaxy of millions of stars, dust, and gas. She recognized the ring around Saturn, and guessed that the largest planet was Jupiter. The tiny planet that was undoubtedly Earth, floated in the blackness. Even from here Kara could see the soft white clouds wrapped around the blue planet—so this was how astronauts saw outer space. It was more beautiful than she could have ever imagined. Streaks of purple and pink painted the black sky, like a modern canvas.

Someone cleared his throat.

Kara turned and gazed into the face of an elderly man. He stood in the middle of the living room between a large sofa and chairs filled with fluffy pillows. The square coffee table beside him was fitted with plates of food and a variety of drinks. The man was of medium height with a round face, pink cheeks, and small sparkling eyes. His white hair brushed his shoulders. A thick beard draped over his large belly. He wore a white kimono with gold stars stitched into the fabric and tied around the waist with a golden belt. Kara thought he looked a lot like Santa Clause. She almost smiled.

The Chief wrinkled his face in a large grin. "Welcome, Kara. I've been expecting you."

The hair on the back of her neck rose. She had heard that voice before. She studied the man more closely, tried to figure where she had heard the voice.

"Come. Have a seat here with me." The Chief gestured to the large beige sofa beside him.

Kara let herself fall into the soft cushions. She got a good look at all the food. A variety of plates were filled with fries, fried chicken, dill pickles, onion rings, hotdogs, pizza, chips, jelly beans, and bottles of soft drinks.

The Chief grabbed a plate from the coffee table and placed it in front of Kara. "Onion ring? They're very good, you know. Very crispy. Here try one —"

Kara shook her head and stared at the plate covered in crispy onion rings. She guessed by the size of the Chief's belly that he could actually eat like a mortal. But how could he?

"No, not really," said the Chief, as though he read her mind. "I don't need food like mortals, but I do enjoy eating from time to time. I can actually taste them. They taste exactly like real food. I rather enjoy eating, you know. Keeps me occupied. You sure you don't want any?"

Kara shook her head again. At last, she recognized the voice. She stared wild-eyed at the man.

"Legan! You're the prisoner from Tartarus!"

The Chief's shoulders shook as he laughed gently. He stuffed three onion rings into his mouth and set the plate down. "Yes. That was me," he said through a mouthful of food.

"So . . . does this mean you knew what would happen? You knew what Asmodeus was planning all along."

"Yes."

Kara stared at him blankly. "I don't understand. If you knew what he was going to do, then why didn't you stop

Zadkiel yourself? Or Asmodeus? Why did you let all those mortals and angels die?"

Sadness passed in the Chief's blue eyes. He was silent for a while. Finally, he spoke. "I wish it were that simple, Kara. But unfortunately it's not. I can impersonate a character here and there ... but I cannot change the course of events. What is meant to happen — will happen. The universe always finds a way. I simply pushed you in the right direction."

"But why me? I'm not even a real angel. I'm tainted with demon. I'm a freak."

The Chief reached over and put two onion rings in his mouth. He wiped the grease from his beard with a white cloth and grabbed a large jar filled with candy.

"Jelly bean?"

Kara shook her head. "No, thank you."

The Chief set the jar on the table. "Asmodeus thought he had created an evil weapon to do his bidding when he used you, but I knew that wasn't the case. He chose you for a purpose, and I chose you for another purpose. You were the only one who could defeat him in the end. He had created his own demise — killed by his own creation — so to speak. You are a special angel, Kara. You saved the world."

Kara remembered the demon lord's wails the first time she had thought she had vanquished him. She had been horrified to learn later, that he had not been destroyed — but simply returned to his demon realm. Perhaps the demon lord couldn't be killed.

"So ... is Asmodeus gone forever? Is he finally dead?"

The Chief picked at some food in his teeth. "He appears to be. Yes, my dear. I believe we have seen the last of him."

It was the good news she'd been waiting to hear. She let herself sink deeper into the soft sofa and tried to relax.

"Then the mortal world will be safe, won't it? If Asmodeus is no longer there to lead the demons, won't they simply disappear? They'll be scattered, leaderless ... and much easier to kill. The mortals will have a demon free world, right?"

"I'm afraid it's not that simple." The Chief shoved a slice of pizza in his mouth, and washed it down with a drink. "Pizza?" He handed her the open cardboard box with the juicy pizza inside.

"Ah—no, thanks. What do you mean?"

The old man placed the box on the seat next to him and clasped his hands in his lap. "Where there is light, there will always be darkness. And where there is good, evil will always linger nearby."

Kara screwed up her face. "I don't get it. What are you saying?"

"There will always be demons, Kara. Just as there will always be angels. Even with Asmodeus's demise, the mortal world will not be safe forever. Soon another angel will fall under the temptation of power, and will want to rule Earth or Horizon. It might be millennia before we know of another demon leader's claim, or it might be in two weeks. We just don't know. And the process will start all over again."

Kara sat back and processed the information. What the Chief said made sense. At least for now, the mortal world and Horizon were safe.

"Kara. I asked you here for a reason. I have a proposition for you."

Kara looked into the Chief's clear blue eyes. "What's your proposition?" She couldn't think of anything. Was he going to send her off on a secret mission?

The Chief ate another onion ring, and Kara couldn't help but stare at his protruding belly. "As you know, I have a few ... vacancies in the archangel department."

Kara sat up straight. She wasn't entirely sure she heard him correctly.

"I'm offering you a chance to be an archangel." The Chief regarded Kara with such intense delight that she figured he was sure she was going to accept. She almost thought about it seriously for a moment. But she knew she couldn't. This wasn't for her.

"You have something different to offer, and your youth will be a healthy change for the government." The Chief's smile broadened and Kara noticed two small dimples below his cheeks. "I believe you would make a great new addition to the council. What do you say, eh?"

His words spun in Kara's head. David's face appeared in her mind's eye. How she missed him. Horizon just wasn't the same without him. She looked up and met the Chief's eyes. What was she to say? How could anyone refuse? But she heard the words in her head before she could actually utter them.

The Chief seemed to be reading her thoughts again. "You are unhappy here, aren't you? I can sense the suffering in your soul, Kara." He placed a hand on her shoulder and squeezed gently. His kind eyes searched her face.

"I'm … I'm sorry — I can't accept." Kara didn't know what else to say. She felt terrible.

"Well then. You give me no choice." The Chief bounced up from the couch. He seemed surprisingly light on his feet for someone so large around the middle. He grabbed a glass of tan liquid and drank the entire contents in one large gulp.

Kara brushed the hair from her eyes. "I beg your pardon?"

"I said … you give me no choice. You give me no choice *but* to offer you something in return. I need to thank you somehow. You have saved my kingdoms — now I will grant you a wish."

Kara stared at him bewildered. "A wish? Are you serious?" He didn't resemble a jinni at all. Maybe Santa could grant wishes too.

"Of course I'm serious, my dear girl. Ask, and it shall be yours."

"Anything?" said Kara to no one in particular.

"Yes," answered the Chief. "I will grant you anything you wish for."

And so Kara smiled for the first time in days.

Chapter 20
A new beginning

Robins chirped and flew in the warm May breezes. Flocks of them fluttered and swooped down onto a manicured lawn. With their red bellies exposed they stood straight and proud. A male robin with his vibrant colors jumped suddenly and poked his beak into the ground. With sharp pulls, the robin yanked a large brown worm from beneath thick layers of grass and swallowed it whole.

Kara smiled. She knew that seeing robins was a sign that summer was near. And that also meant school was nearly over. She could finally concentrate fully on her presentation package for the Dawson College art program that started in the fall. Her work needed to be outstanding to qualify for the program. They accepted only the best, and Kara believed that she was one of them. Her high school teachers had praised her strange demonic-looking paintings. They told her she had raw talent, and they believed she had a real chance to be accepted.

Kara breathed in the fresh warm air through her bedroom window. A few clouds peppered the blue sky. Kara imagined them to be great big eagles chasing each other across the sky.

The robins fluttered away. A young couple walked up the street holding hands. They kissed and the girl giggled excitedly. Kara watched them with longing in her heart. They were disgustingly happy in love. It oozed off them as they stared into each other's eyes. Her ache deepened. How she wished it were her. Although she was seventeen now, she was still unmistakably single. She wished to find that special someone some day, hopefully before she turned forty. She watched the young couple disappear around the corner.

Kara let out a long sigh. She wouldn't let her feelings get in the way of this perfect day. She'd have tomorrow to feel sorry for herself, she decided. Kara laughed. It was a beautiful day; a perfect day to spend outside on a park bench and read a great book. Saturdays were ideal for going down to the used bookstore she loved. She thought maybe a nice book on birds would do — or maybe that hardcover edition of *The Wizard of Oz* she'd been dying to get a hold of.

But that wasn't the only reason she wanted to go to the bookstore. She needed a job. She had to save money to go to college, and she figured she might as well get a job she'd enjoy. Besides, she practically lived at that bookstore; it was like a second home to her. And Mr. Patterson had kindly insinuated that he needed help the other day. Kara decided that *she* would be the one to help.

She pushed off the window-sill and skipped over to her closet. She pulled open the doors and poked her head in.

"Mom! Where's my black shirt!" yelled Kara from inside her closet. "I can't find it anywhere? You said you washed it."

"It's in the dryer," Kara heard her mother's muffled voice coming from the kitchen.

After a few minutes of rummaging through the dryer, Kara pulled out her favorite black v-neck t-shirt. It was more like dark grey now, she realized, but she didn't care. It was the most comfortable shirt she owned. She covered her face in it and sniffed. She smiled. It smelled like lavender. She pulled the shirt over her head and dashed towards the kitchen.

Her mother stood by the sink. She stared out the window while she did the dishes. Her face looked peaceful. Her large brown eyes sparkled, and somehow she looked younger. Maybe it was the way the sun illuminated her face. It must be that.

On her tip-toes, she leaned over and kissed her mother on the cheek. "I'll see you later. Gotta go." Kara sprinted out of the kitchen and headed towards the front door.

Her mother turned. "What? Where are you going?" Greasy water dripped from her hands on the black and white linoleum floors. "Will you be back for supper, Kara?" She called and wiped her hands on her jeans.

Kara pulled open the front door. "I don't know. Going to the bookstore. Love ya!" she called back, and closed the door behind her.

She flew down the two flights of stairs, through a small dingy lobby, and finally out through the apartment building's front door. Glad to be out of the stinky cigarette smell from the lobby, Kara breathed in the sweet aroma of the two lilac trees that stood by her building. The deep purple blooms gave off a rich sent. She would cut a few branches for her mom when she got back. They were her mother's favorite. Warm air brushed her cheeks. She breathed it all in.

Kara strolled down the sidewalk and crossed to Saint-Marc Street. Shoppers already scurried up the street with large bags dangling from their arms. Everywhere she looked shops lined the streets. Green, red, blue, and yellow doors stood ajar, inviting the curious shoppers in. Paul's Pet Shop came into view, and Kara stopped to admire the golden retriever puppies in the bay window. As usual, the window next to it demanded her attention.

The large metal cage took up the entire bay window. Inside the cage was a small brown monkey with a shriveled black face like a dried plum. It was the same monkey she'd passed everyday on her way to school, and on her way to the bookstore. His yellow eyes always gave her the creeps. It was as though he was trying to communicate something to her. The monkey was the owner's pet, and everyday he would place the cage in one of the two bay windows at the front of the shop. Strangely enough, the monkey would spend the day making obscene gestures to the passersby. At first, Kara thought he was cute and friendly, so she had poked her fingers through the bars to pet him — and had yanked them back quickly — after he had bitten them. She never cared for him since.

And now he climbed up the walls of his metal prison and pushed his face between the metal bars, screeching at Kara, demanding her attention once again.

"What is it with you and your bad attitude?" said Kara to the monkey. "You know, if you tried to be a little nicer, I might give you some chips." Kara tapped her front pocket.

The monkey's wet yellow eyes glared at her. He squished his little face into a scowl. He pursed his lips — and spit.

Kara stepped out of the way. The spit splashed onto the sidewalk. Kara laughed. She had recognized his spit-face, since he had spit on her before. She had told herself then that she would never let him do that to her again. Now she had been prepared. Soon, she would get him back.

"You see? Now why did you go and do that? You nasty little bugger." The monkey seemed angry that he had missed her and started to howl and rattle his cage.

Crazy beast, Kara smiled as she passed by his cage, ignoring his wild tantrums.

The smell of burning incense filled her nose. Kara looked to a great red door that was kept open by a tall stack of books. A peeling wooden sign with painted red letters read, *Old Jim's Bookstore* — her new employer.

With a grin Kara leaped onto the street, her eyes glued on the bookstore, and ran into someone.

She jumped back and yelped in surprise. She looked up. A handsome young man stared back at her. He had disheveled blonde hair, a gorgeous face and strong square jaw. A brown leather jacket covered his strong shoulders. He wore a pair of shabby blue jeans with a white t-shirt. His was fit, an athlete, Kara thought. He regarded her with piercing blue eyes, the kind that forced Kara to look away.

"Sorry," said the stranger with an amused grin. "Didn't see you there."

Kara's heart caught in her throat. Where had she heard that voice before? Her eyes went to his face again. Goose bumps spread over her entire body. She started to shake. That face looked familiar to her. Who was he? She couldn't stop staring, and when the stranger smiled at her, she looked away abashed. Her cheeks burned. She knew she was blushing.

"Do I know you?" The stranger took a step forward. "You look really familiar. Have we met?"

Kara's jaw was glued shut. She couldn't speak. Her skin tingled.

Kara stared into the face of the young man she had just met, but somehow she felt she'd known him all her life. It was as if he had come from another life at a different time. She felt the blood rush to her face again, but she didn't care. She couldn't keep her eyes off him. She couldn't understand what was happening.

"How can I forget such a babe?" The stranger raked his fingers through his hair. "Man, this is going to sound really weird … but … I feel as if I know you. I've seen your face before. But it feels like more than that — like I've known you all my life." He scratched the back of his neck and laughed softly. Color flushed his cheeks. "Whoa. I sound crazy."

Kara clasped her trembling hands behind her back. "You're not crazy. I … I … feel the same as you, as if I know you already," she said finally. "This *is* pretty weird."

The stranger sighed in relief. He threw out his hand. "I'm David … and apparently a little crazy."

David, Kara repeated in her head. Somehow she already knew his name. She pressed her hand in his. "I'm Kara."

David squeezed her hand gently, but didn't let go. His skin was warm, and Kara felt shivers down her spine. His touch was electrifying. Kara flinched involuntarily. Her heart pounded painfully against her chest. She was sure David could hear it. But he still didn't let go of her hand.

"Kara," David repeated and stared at her. He stood there searching her face, and Kara was frozen in his gaze, but unwilling to move, for fear she would wake up from this dream. It was a dream, wasn't it?

David shifted his weight. "Are you going somewhere, Kara?"

Kara's mouth opened, but no words come out. Embarrassed, she clamped her jaw shut again. She felt David's warm fingers press against her skin. Somehow it felt natural to her. After a moment, she gently removed her hand from David's grip and pointed to the bookstore. "There ... I'm going—I was going to the bookstore."

David looked over to the bookstore and then back to her. "Mind if I come with you? I'm not much of a reader, but something's telling me not to let you out of my sight. Like I need to keep you safe."

Kara's heart skipped a beat. Something was telling her the same thing. A powerful feeling to watch over him came over her suddenly. It didn't make sense, she knew. How could this be happening? But she didn't' care. This felt right. David felt right. She couldn't explain it. It was a feeling deep inside her. She knew she was supposed to be with him.

Kara smiled up at him. "Sure. But I'm positive I can find something for you to read."

David chuckled softly. "I doubt it. Reading's really not my thing—I'm more of a video game kinda guy."

"I had a feeling you'd say that."

David kept eyeing Kara with a cocky expression plastered all over his face, as though he had won a prize. She rather enjoyed his attentions, even if they were a little overconfident. Somehow Kara felt complete.

They crossed the street together.

Kara smiled.

This was the best day of her life.

DON'T MISS THE NEXT EXCITING ADVENTURE IN THE
SOUL GUARDIANS SERIES

NETHERWORLD

Chapter I
Old Jim's Bookstore

Kara inhaled deeply and blew the dust off a row of books with cracked covers and ripped spines. The air smelled like a mixture of old glue and mildew. The dust motes hovered like a swarm of insects, and the hot and humid damp lingered and clung to her clothes. It was not the perfect environment to stow old books, but she loved how the smell of ink and paper seeped out. It was the smell of imagination — where great minds came together and created magic with their words — the smell of adventures not yet discovered. In books, anything was possible...and she loved it.

She wiped the perspiration from her forehead and pulled her hair into a ponytail. She squeezed *The Adventures of Huckleberry Finn* between *The Call of the Wild* and *The Old Man and the Sea*, in the classic novels section. She nudged them into a perfect straight line, with their spines arranged vertically. Once satisfied with her work, she wiped the moisture and dirt from her hands onto her blue jeans, adding to the layer of grime from the day's work. The ladder creaked and wobbled under her weight. She clasped her hands firmly around the rail and stepped down carefully. Once she reached the bottom, she jumped the last step.

With a smile on her face Kara pushed a metal trolley piled with books and magazines toward the front of the shop. She ducked under the single light bulb that flickered nervously from a loose wire in the center of the shop and drove the trolley between crooked stacks of books that wiggled all the way up to the ceiling in some places and teetered perilously.

Rays of light spilled through a large bay window from the front of the shop and illuminated the bookshelves in a soft golden glow. Dust particles glowed in the light like miniature snowflakes. Kara could see the grey cobwebs that draped from the highest corners of the ceiling and made a mental note to sweep them later with her broom. Brown and beige striped wallpaper peeled from the walls behind a fragile wooden counter that lined the right side of the shop. An old cash register with manual buttons and a red lever sat above it. Below the cash register was a glass case displaying different sizes of crystal balls. Kara giggled at her distorted reflections in them. A warm breeze brushed Kara's bangs from her face. Wind chimes sang faintly from above the open front door.

Kara sneezed. The trolley jerked. A thick blanket of dust covered most of the back bookshelves, a clear indication that she still had a lot of cleaning to do. It would take weeks to dust the shop free from years of neglect. She seriously doubted it had ever been clean to begin with. On her very first day at the shop,

Kara had given the windows a good cleaning and had swept and scraped the floors of dingy brown grime and maroon stains that she'd rather not think about.

Kara gladly inhaled the summer wind from the open door — dandelions and freshly cut lawns — her spirits lifted with each new smell. It was an awesome feeling. School was over, and she was now officially an employee in a place she loved and for a man she admired. Mr. Patterson had given her a summer job in his bookstore. Her duties were to help him categorize all the new books into a new computer program, to keep the shop clean, and to work the cash register when he was on his lunch break. It had proven to be the best job ever. And Kara was determined to save enough money for the first semester at Dawson College. Mr. Patterson even told her that he would keep her on part time when she went to school. She couldn't ask for a better boss or a better job. At last, things were finally looking up for her.

With the trolley parked, she grabbed a handful of *National Geographic* magazines and placed them by corresponding dates along the middle shelf from the magazine rack. She shuffled them together — and froze.

Her hair stood on end. Kara inexplicably sensed a presence. She followed the source of the feeling towards the bay window —

Someone was staring at her from across the street.

Her heart hammered against her chest. A young girl in an old fashioned white dress with a large red bow tied at the middle, stared at Kara from the opposite side of the street. Her silky black hair was cut short at her jaw line and accentuated her sharp features. She was beautiful, like an expensive doll. She looked to be about twelve years old. Even from the distance, Kara could see traces of redness around her eyes and nose. Her pallid face was pulled into a grimace, her eyes wide in terror. Kara could almost feel her panic. Her eyes pleaded for help, for Kara's help. An inexplicable connection with the girl rose in Kara's chest. It was as though they were related somehow, like a long lost cousin. The girl jerked her head around suddenly and started to back away.

Two men in meticulously tailored grey suits approached the young girl from either side. Their platinum hair and faces were identical and their skin was a sickly white color like that of diseased albinos. They moved swiftly and with purpose. The girl backed up against the front wall of the neighboring shop. She locked eyes with Kara once more in a silent plea. She mouthed the words *Help me*. Kara held her breath. The girl was trapped between the two leering men with black eyes. The loud hammering of Kara's heart in her ears drowned out all other sounds around her. The little girl was no match for these two evil looking men. Kara had to do something, she had to try to help her.

Kara pushed the trolley out of her way and threw herself over the counter. She grabbed the baseball bat, which Mr. Patterson kept hidden behind the counter in case of a perilous transaction with a customer, and dashed out of the bookstore and onto the street.

She skidded to a stop.

It was empty. The girl had vanished and so had the black-eyed men. The street rang with silence. The sidewalk was bare except for a few pigeons pecking at the ground.

Were her eyes playing tricks on her again? Was this another strange vision? For the past few months she'd had the sensation of being watched. She had perceived creepy shadows in dark places following her every move, lashing out at her when they thought she wasn't looking. But as soon as she would turn around to confront whatever they were, the shadows would disappear in a blink of an eye. Perhaps this was one of those occurrences. Or perhaps she was going mad. She thought it must be the latter.

"Are you planning on beating someone with that bat?"

Kara whirled around. David stood here, handsome as always, with his customary cheeky grin and tousled blond hair. With his head in the air, he sauntered toward her with a hop in his step.

"Is it safe? Or should I come back later?" laughed David, and he jammed his hands in his pockets.

Kara ignored him and watched the opposite side of the street. "I—I thought I saw something."

David raised his brows. "And so you decided to go all *vigilante* and grabbed a baseball bat—to beat it with?"

"I saw a girl. I think she was in trouble—no, she *was* in trouble. She was really scared and needed my help." Kara's knuckles turned white as she grasped the bat tightly. She remembered the little girl's petrified face as she retreated from the approaching men.

"What girl?" David searched the street. "I don't see any girl. Are you sure you saw something? You know, all that dust you inhale all day could be affecting your brain."

Kara sighed and lowered the bat. "She was there a minute ago. I'm sure of it. And there were these two weird looking men...with white hair—really ugly looking and creepy—I felt they were going to hurt her. They had these scary black eyes."

"Black eyes? As though they were punched in the face or something? Just as you were about to do with that bat, right?"

Kara looked into David's puzzled face and decided to drop it. Clearly he thought she was mad. She shook her head and shrugged. "Never mind." She gave out a frustrated breath and then gave him a lopsided smile. "What are you doing here so early anyway? I thought you had soccer practice?"

"I did." David did some fancy foot-work to impress Kara. "It got cancelled. I thought we could catch an afternoon movie or something."

Kara tried hard not to smile, but her face betrayed her. She looked quickly away from David. Her cheeks burned, and she knew instantly her face had gone tomato red. Her heart pounded in her ears.

"Um…let me ask Mr. Patterson first. He might still need me for the rest of the day." She hoped silently that he wouldn't. David had been coming around the shop every day since the very first time they had accidentally met two months ago. And every time he came around butterflies fluttered inside her belly.

With the baseball bat loose at her side, Kara walked back into the shop. David ducked below the wind chime and followed behind her. She heard the click of the back door as it closed. She looked up as Mr. Patterson shuffled towards them, his bones creaking as he approached. He scratched his head, sending ripples through his wispy white hair. His short legs peeked out from under his usual khaki Bermuda shorts and colorful yellow and orange Hawaiian shirt. The floor-boards creaked under the weight of his bare feet. Kara never understood why he walked around barefoot in the grime and dust on the floors. But as time went on, she got used to seeing his large square toes and long yellow nails. She reminded herself to get him a gift certificate at the local spa, *Toes with Bows*, for a pedicure. If she was forced to look at his feet, then at least they could be groomed.

Mr. Patterson waved at them excitedly. "Why, hello, Denis! What brings you to this side of the literary world? Have you come to buy a book at last? There's a great new section on adventure books for boys over there—" He flung his long white beard over his shoulder and pointed to a tall book shelf to his left.

David smiled uncomfortably and scratched the back of his neck. "Uh...no, Mr. P—but thanks anyway. I'm sure they're all...swell." David turned to Kara and whispered under his breath. "He's still calling me *Denis*." Kara covered her mouth and laughed.

Mr. Patterson halted and watched Kara warily. "Clara? Why are you holding the *mad-bat*? Did something happen? Were you engaged in combat with a psychotic customer?"

"Un, no, I was just..."

David snorted. "The mad-bat? Seriously? Sounds a little *batty* to me—"

Kara kicked David in the shin and hid the baseball bat behind her back. "Uh...nothing. I was just...cleaning it." She walked over to the counter and placed the bat behind it.

"Actually, Mr. P," said David, "I came to see if Kara could get the rest of the afternoon off."

"I see." Mr. Patterson eyed David suspiciously for a moment. His clear blue eyes peered out from under the folds of hundreds of wrinkles. He pursed his lips and scratched his head. "Well, I don't see why not. I think Clara's done quite enough today already. You can go with Denis if it pleases you."

Excitement rushed through Kara's breast. She dashed back. "Really? Thank you, Mr. Patterson. You're too good to me."

"Nonsense." Mr. Patterson waved a dismissive hand. He stood silent for a moment, his face perplexed. "Dear me. I can't remember what I was about to do just now...my mind seems to wander on its own as I get older. A very strange business, this old age." His blue eyes glazed over, and he stared into space.

Kara peeked at David and then back at Mr. Patterson. "Mr. Patterson—if you want, I can stay and help you find what you were looking for. Really it's fine. I can go to the movies another time. I'm sure *David* won't mind." Kara gave David a sidelong glance.

"No, no. That won't be necessary, my dear. You go on now with David. I'm sure whatever it was…it'll turn up soon enough." Mr. Patterson waddled over behind the counter. He slid open the glass compartment door from which he pulled a fist-sized crystal ball. Specks of light reflected off his face, and he gazed at it intensely without blinking. He held it with both hands and was still.

"Mr. Patterson? Are you all right?" asked Kara. And when he didn't answer, she asked again. "Are you feeling okay? You seem a little pale. Can I get you a glass of water?"

"The guy's a little spaced out…if you know what I mean," whispered David beside her. He whirled his finger at the side of his head and opened his eyes wide.

Kara ignored David and studied the old man. She lowered her voice. "He does that sometimes. Whenever he stares into one of those crystal balls—it seems he forgets the world around him. It's as if he's off somewhere else. It's pretty…freaky."

"Maybe he's got the early signs of Alzheimer's."

Kara shook her head irritably. "No, he doesn't. He's just...old. I'd like to see you at his age — see how you would handle yourself."

"I'd be the sexiest old fart in town, baby. All the single senior ladies would be chasing me with their canes. I'd be awesome."

Kara rolled her eyes and laughed. "You're such a moron." She watched the old man somberly. It pained her to see him so distraught. "I hate to leave him here like this, though. What if someone comes in...and he's still staring into that ball, and he doesn't answer them? They might call the police or something. What if they lock him up?"

David squeezed her shoulder gently. "Don't worry. The old dude had this shop long before you came along. I'm sure he'll be fine. Let's go. The movie starts in half an hour."

"I hope so." Reluctantly, Kara turned around and followed David towards the door. "So... what movie did you want to see? Please don't say another zombie film. I think I've seen enough blood and guts to last me a lifetime."

David cracked his knuckles and grinned. "I was thinking the new —"

"Wait! Stop!"

With a crash, Mr. Patterson's crystal ball exploded into a million pieces as it hit the floor. He ignored it and ran wildly towards them. His white hair bounced from the top of his head, and Kara couldn't help but be reminded of the little luck-trolls with wispy purple hair she used to collect. He waved his hands frantically in the air. "You cannot leave. The darkness comes. The legion needs you. The mortals are in danger!"

David whistled softly. "Whoa...and you said the old fart wasn't nuts? He just poured a bucket of crazy on us —"

"Hang on," said Kara, cutting him off. "Something's wrong. I've never seen him so agitated."

After a moment, Mr. Patterson stood before them. His eyes were wide and crazed. He pulled at his hair with trembling hands. "I have seen it! It is time. You must go back!"

Kara searched his face. His big blue eyes were lost under bushy white brows.

"Time for what? You're not making any sense." Her body stiffened. What if he had gone mad? She would have to look for another job. A lump formed in her throat. She looked over at David who raised his brows.

Mr. Patterson paced on the spot. "The time is now. You must prepare yourselves. They are waiting for you. You must leave the mortal world."

Kara wiped the sweat from her forehead with her hand. It was getting worse by the minute. "Who's waiting? I don't understand. Mr. Patterson, you're not making any sense —"

"Keys! I almost forgot!" The old man rushed over to the counter, rummaged through a drawer, and rocketed back. Two golden key cards glimmered in his hands. He held them up to

Kara and David. "Here—you must take your cards. You cannot enter level five without them."

David laughed and took one of the keys. "Thanks, Mr. P—maybe you should sit down and relax a little. Whoa…is this real gold?"

Kara shoved David aside and shook Mr. Patterson gently by the shoulders. "Mr. Patterson. You're scaring me. I think you need to lie down and have a glass of water. Did you eat something today?"

Mr. Patterson nodded impatiently. "Yes, yes, of course." He grabbed her hand and placed the other golden key card in her palm. He curled her fingers around it. "Kept it safe. You will need it. It's only a matter of seconds now."

Kara blinked the moisture from her eyes. "Okay. That's it. I'm going to lock up and take you home. We're not going to the movies anymore."

She started for the door, but Mr. Patterson grabbed her arm forcefully and pulled her back to face him.

"No! It's happening. You cannot go anywhere. You must stay here. Both of you."

Kara and David shared a look. She realized this was a lot worse than she had first anticipated. She would have to call someone. She decided to phone her mother. Her mother would know what to do.

"I need to use your phone."

"No!" Mr. Patterson grabbed Kara by the elbow and steered her back to face him. "There isn't time. It comes now. Prepare yourselves."

"What's coming?" laughed David, playing along. "The darkness? Will it give us more gold cards?"

The old man backed away from them suddenly and pointed towards the ceiling. His eyes were wide in fear. "The earthquake," he whispered.

Kara frowned. "The earthquake? We don't get earthquakes here—"

As if on cue, the bookshelves started to rattle and the ground shook fiercely. An enormous boom thundered around them, as though the earth itself had split open. Bookshelves swayed dangerously, spilling out their contents. Books toppled over and crashed onto the floor around them. The walls cracked, revealing large gaping holes. Chunks of plaster cascaded down from the ceiling and covered Kara and David in a blanket of white dust. Kara coughed as the powder burned her throat.

"Kara! This way!" David yanked Kara by the arm and pulled her towards the counter. They ducked and flung themselves against the wood frame to protect themselves from the falling rubble as best as they could.

Kara looked around nervously. "Where's Mr. Patterson?" she shouted over the groans and creaks of falling debris.

A huge chunk of plaster crashed on the floor, just inches away from them.

"I don't know!" yelled David. He inspected the ceiling for more falling boulders. "The ceiling is coming down. We'll get crushed if we stay here. We have to get out of here now!"

Kara nodded and followed David out from behind the counter. They ducked and jumped out of the way of broken shelves and dangerously sharp chunks of rock —

BOOM!

Half the ceiling came down behind them. The counter disappeared under an avalanche of wreckage.

Kara watched David's lips move, but she couldn't hear what he was saying. All she could hear was the hammering of her heart and the thundering crash of falling debris. He pointed to the door and grabbed her hand.

Desperately they ran for the door. It was near. They were almost at the threshold —

An earsplitting crack vibrated around them.

The remaining ceiling tumbled down.

Kara's last image was of a brick wall crashing on top of her. A tremendous weight pressed on her chest, and then her consciousness left.

About the Author

Kim Richardson is the author of the SOUL GUARDIANS series. She was born in a small town in Northern Quebec, Canada, and studied in the field of 3D Animation. As an Animation Supervisor for a VFX company, Kim worked on big Hollywood films and stayed in the field of animation for 14 years. Since then, she has retired from the VFX world and settled in the country where she writes fulltime.

To learn more about Kim Richardson, visit:

www.kim-richardson.blogspot.com
www.facebook.com/KRAuthorPage
http://twitter.com/Kim_Richardson_

CPSIA information can be obtained at www.ICGtesting.com
Printed in the USA
BVOW04s1128060414

349890BV00008B/142/P